Half of all proceeds from this book
are donated to Chicago Public Schools.

They need it.

The Fairytale Chicago
of
Francesca of Finnegan

www.fairytalechicago.com
@fairytalechicago

Ordering Information:

Quantity sales. Special discounts are available on quantity purchases by bookstores, corporations, associations, and others. For details, contact the publisher at the email address above.

Orders by U.S. trade bookstores and wholesalers may also order directly from Ingram Spark.

ISBN: 978-0-9981492-1-9

Warning

Content may be deemed offensive by Polish Indians, vice presidents of something, my wife, Finbar Finnegan's wife, LinkedIn, little kids who think this book is for little kids, Thumbelina, Brown Liners, mermaids, and the wind.

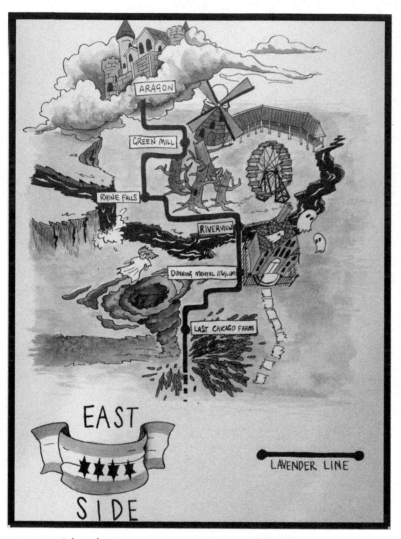

Asking how to get anyvere on zis map is like asking vere to fall down a rabbit hole, or how to valk srough a looking glass

I

"God save the bachelors, the bachelors of finance.
They've spent all their gold on golden underpants."

The Starry Night

Fairyism

There *is* magic in the city.

When Rich Lyons was a little boy, he learned of the magic from an old, cockeyed, Captain Hook–looking magician. The old man sat alone at a table for two outside a neighborhood bar every summer day, all day, always with a glass of twinkling whiskey. He said the twinkle had once been in his eye, but had blown out one windy day and splashed right into the whiskey. Rich liked how the twinkle twinkled in the whiskey. He liked it so much, he asked the old man if he could have it. The man told Rich he didn't need it, because he already had a twinkle of his own, and besides, that particular twinkling whiskey tasted like shit, worse than Malört[1], if that's possible.

"You be careful," the old man warned, "because in the city of wind, a twinkle may blow out. The wind here, it twirls and sings like a music-box ballerina. It plays tricks and tells stories like an old-man magician. Like me, like this …"

And so, the old man performed tricks for Rich and

---

[1] *Disgusting alcoholic spirit, occupied by the evil spirit of a bootlegger, who was bootlegged himself. Available only in Chicago.*

regaled him with city folklore and fantasy. He said the Great Chicago Fire was arson, started by a fire-breathing dragon from the Fulton River District who was fed up with the cold winters. He said the Chicago River started flowing backward when a giant sea serpent sneezed so powerfully, it changed the direction of the current. He said the sky was purple (not black) above the city because a wicked witch had stolen all the black for her cats and bats and witch hats.

Rich's favorite story was one about the L trains, and how each had come to be named for a color. The old man said the colors arrived when the first skyscrapers did. Before then, all the trains were the same dull brown. On the day the first skyscraper went up, a rainbow, unused to encountering buildings so high in the sky, accidentally crashed into it. When the rainbow crashed, each of its individual colors went splattering in all directions. Some landed on the L trains and stained them. The only train to miss a color was the Brown Line, because, the old man said, it was offline for repairs.

The old man also said there was one line, a secret line, that got a splash of lavender.

One day, Rich asked the old man if he could use his magic to tell fortunes. The old man said, well, hell, of course he could, it was a matter of simple city magic. Rich asked if he might hear his own fortune. He wanted to know what he would be when he grew up.

The old man told Rich there wasn't much he *wouldn't* be when he grew up. He would be a father, a husband, an uncle, a brother, a friend. He would be a ghost in the graveyard. He would be a vice president of something. He would be a pisser in the pancake batter. He would be a reveler-adventurer. He would be a hider and seeker. He would be a rocket man. A businessman.

And, he would be a rich man.

The Prodigal Businessman, or the proportions of the human body
according to a senior vice president of something

Richard the Rich

Rich as in wealthy, not as in the name. He hadn't been the name Rich since he was that boy with the twinkle. He'd grown *way* out of the twinkle, and into Richard K. Lyons, fine specimen of a businessman, proudly registered as such on LinkedIn. His was a hugely popular profile on LinkedIn. He was a demigod of LinkedIn. He had his initials stitched into the cuffs of all his dress shirts as proof of his demigod status, for all the world to behold. He had even more initials, things like CPA, CFA, and CFP, listed on his fabulously expensive, platinum-engraved business cards. He stored those cards within an Italian leather iPhone case, along with exactly one-half gram of cocaine. The cocaine was something of a performance-enhancing drug, helping Richard in his job as one of those accomplished vice presidents of something—maybe marketing, accounting, finance, sales, or maybe all of them. It didn't matter. The important thing was that Richard was a master and commander of commerce and capitalism.

Richard was rich.

Richard lived with his beautiful wife and young son just

outside the city, in an affluent suburb. He was neighbors with other affluents who tasted craft beer on weekends. Some even brewed it. "There is no such thing as too much hops in a beer," Richard would drunkenly proclaim. He'd drink nothing but the hoppiest hops brewed by the most esteemed hopsmen. The only time he made an exception was at his annual fraternity reunion, where he would force down one watery Keystone Light—"For old time's sake"—then ten more after that.

Richard was a hopper of hops, nobleman of the landed aristocracy, family man, businessman, vice president of something, master and commander. To suggest a man of such wealth and title could be unhappy might seem unthinkable, yet Richard was just that, and there were many reasons.

First, Richard's marriage was on the verge of collapse. He cheated on his wife as often as he possibly could, for no other reason than that he could, and she of course despised him for it. He was a middle-stage alcoholic. His once sporadic cocaine use had turned into a serious addiction. He was unhealthy. He was shaped like a bottle of Red Stripe beer. He was pre-diabetic. He was generally dishonest, insincere, greedy, narcissistic, decadent, and dissatisfied. It's true he was professionally successful, but he hated his career as the vice president of something. Without his many respectable bank accounts, he might have spontaneously combusted. There was little else to the man.

The world was all dark for Richard, but it hadn't always been so. The story of how things darkened is complicated, and starts when Richard was born, on the Northwest Side of the city, one of too many siblings within a too-small garden-unit apartment, located under one of those dime-a-dozen, three-flat brick walkups. The apartment was tiny, only a little larger than affluent Richard's master bedroom and bath. It was tiny because the family had no money. Richard was raised by a single mother who earned next to nothing as a tollbooth attendant. His father, who had died when little Rich was in the fourth grade, had been a janitor. On his father's death certificate, "chronic cirrhosis of the liver / alcoholism" was listed as the cause, though it was only a good guess, as there had never been an autopsy. His mother couldn't afford it. His father left the family with nothing to pay for an autopsy, a funeral, or a grave. So they scattered his ashes in the Chicago River, near the former site of the Riverview Amusement Park, where his father had played as a boy. There on the riverside, little Rich carved his father's initials into a weeping willow tree, as deeply as he could slice. He figured it was better than having no grave at all.

Nothing came easily for Richard. He was born into nothing. He would have to work hard for anything considerably better, and with little help. All he had in his favor was a drive to do something, inspired by all the nothing. In that way, his story was not so uncommon, but only in that way.

Richard found his first job young, and worked and worked and worked. Then he played and played and played, to balance things out. One night, he even played with a fairy, though he normally played with the many friends he'd made early in life, within his neighborhood. He kept most of those connections over the years. He was a better friend than family man. His friends revered him. Richard the conversationalist! He had a lot to say and a way of saying it. Got the gift of gab from his ancestors across the water. He was clever, the wingman who did all the flying. It was said he could get your grandfather laid. Your *dead* grandfather. And there was an adventurous heart in him, wasn't there? Yes, there was.

Richard the adventurer!

Well, adventure-seeker, at least. Few genuine adventures were still available to his generation, that cohort of people born in the late seventies and early eighties, in the gray area between Generation X and Millennial. There were no great wars to be won, frontiers to be explored, historic causes to fight for. So his youthful adventures became the next best thing: a series of nights spent in the most drunken, pixilated[2] oblivion imaginable. Richard and his friends became consummate professionals at this type of adventure. What wishes they'd wished into their wishing wells as children were washed away one night by a tidal wave of piss and puke and hangovers, the byproducts of some truly epic adventure. Few of Richard's friends would finish high school without at least one chemical addiction, but they hardly noticed it. They were too busy adventuring!

The college years were the most adventurous.

One particular college adventure took place within the

---

[2] *Origin mid-19ᵗʰ century, variant of pixie-led / to be led astray by pixies, figuratively "confused," literally "fucked up."*

twenty-eight-story orgy of Abercrombie & Fitch that was Richard's college dormitory. Late one spring afternoon, the dormitory was evacuated, ahead of an approaching weather system thought to contain tornadoes. Earlier that day, Richard and his friends had boldly smuggled a barrel of Keystone Light within a garbage can up to their twenty-sixth-floor room, where a glorious party of spiky hair and beer bongs ensued. As the skies blackened and the alarms sounded in the hallways, some among the less-adventurous evacuated, but not the core of the adventurers, not Richard. He stood by the window, intoxicated, entranced by the surreal sight of passing funnel clouds. Within one storm cloud, Richard saw a little girl in a white dress flailing here and there in the wind. He couldn't believe it. Her blonde hair looked like the tail of a kite. Richard recognized her, and he couldn't believe that either. He knew the flying girl from an adventure he'd once had. Or was it a dream he'd once had? The girl was a queen of wherever it was. But he lost sight of the flying queen, and soon forgot her entirely, after a certain special girl snuck up from behind and distracted him. The certain special girl whispered lyrics in Richard's ear from a Cars song playing in the background.

I see you under the midnight

Love darts in your eyes

How far can you take it

Till you realize

There's magic in your eyes?

Then they all played Twister, naked.

When Richard wasn't playing Twister in a twister, he was majoring in finance. Finance seemed like a practical career path for someone who came from zero finances. He supposed he might obtain finances with the finance degree. He thought he might get a respectable, stable job at a bank or other corporation. He thought he might be a man of business. Although he was bored with the subject matter of the finance classes themselves, he performed well in them. He graduated, and before he knew it had become the businessman he'd hoped to be, working during the day, wrapping up his MBA at night. The MBA seemed like a practical evolution for the businessman. After he finished the MBA, he paid his professional dues by working grueling hours doing something seemingly important in an office, through his mid-twenties, until one day, he became the vice president of something.

Then came the family. Richard's family began one stormy midsummer night under the shelter of a crowded beer tent at one of those city street festivals. There, Richard met a girl named Erin, a friend of a friend, who stood out from all the other friends of friends. The two dated for only a few months before they decided to marry. Richard would justify this haste to his friends by claiming he was getting old, and of the age when you must marry whomever you happen to be dating. That was only partially true. He also loved her. Together, they would have a son named Andy. Richard was truly happy after the boy was born, but only for a short time. There remained a conspicuous hole in an odd little corner of Richard's heart, which he could never manage to fill. He couldn't say how the hole had gotten there, but it was there, like a lost memory, pleading to be found.

The transition from single man to settled man went poorly for Richard. He became restless. Home life didn't suit him. Diapers didn't suit him. And through all the major changes in his life, including the new family, his worst habits persisted. He could never reconcile the adventurer with the family man. The adventures actually intensified after his son was born. At the end of a long workweek, he rarely returned home until Saturday or Sunday. He found himself wandering through the city with like-minded friends or co-workers or girlfriends, sometimes for days. The first time he failed to return home after work on a Friday night, his wife reported him missing—but only that first time. She worried where he was after that, but refused to be made a fool again.

She would not report someone missing who chose to go missing.

***

To many, the story of Richard's rise to corporate greatness from the garden unit was the stuff of American Dreams. "Richard is so driven!" people would say. "Richard has a beautiful family. What's his son's name? Andy? Beautiful name. Andy. Rolls off the tongue. How *is* his mother? Great that Richard has finally settled down. You know he was once a crazy, wild thing. Oh, yes, wild *and* crazy. I swear he was! But that was long ago. Tell the Lyons family we said hello." And so on.

Richard knew better, and was depressed for knowing better. His life had become stuck in a sad, uninteresting cycle of work and play, broken up by the expected Life Events. It was a cycle Richard recognized there was no breaking out of. He developed a dark, fatalistic view of his life, in which everything that was to happen already had, and he was powerless to change his destiny. Everything had become a known eventuality, to the point where at times, he felt his own self-awareness slipping away. He was transforming into an expensively dressed zombie, numb to the misery of his daily routine. The numbness seemed to accelerate the passing of time. He noticed this with an emotionless curiosity. His misery caused the seasons to fly by, so that he found himself always on the brink of the coldest Chicago winter.

Richard might have been able to manage some of his problems, if not for his career. It was the career that damaged him most. He'd worked half his life doing jobs he hated to get a job he hated. But he'd made it. Hadn't he? After all, he was the vice president of something. Someday, he might be senior vice president!

Or not.

He would rather have been crushed to death by a giant, falling skyscraper icicle. Which actually happens, by the way. Consider this article, from the *Tribune*:

A suburban man waiting for his son to finish a college entrance exam was killed Tuesday when a chunk of ice fell from a four-story building downtown and hit him in the head. Matthew Radowski, 49, of Plainfield, was waiting for a cab in front of the building, at 535 N. Michigan Ave., around 10:30 a.m. when a piece of ice described by one police officer as "the size of a microwave" snapped off the south end of the building's Michigan Avenue facade and landed on him. Falling ice is something of a routine wintertime hazard around the canyons of Chicago's downtown office buildings and high-rises.

To most mortals, a lethal shard of falling ice would probably sound terrifying. But it was inviting to Richard. There were days when Richard didn't mind the thought of being crushed to death by a microwave-size ice chunk. One of those days occurred, appropriately, in the middle of winter.

It was a Friday.

Caution, Falling MIce

The Brown Line to Auschwitz

The Friday started no differently from any other. Richard took the Brown Line downtown to his place of business. For those who don't know, the Brown Line is a ramshackle, barely functioning rail train built over one hundred years ago. It looks and operates as if its last tune-up occurred over one hundred years ago. The Brown Line is one of those color-coded trains that make up the greater Chicago L system, coursing through the city's anatomy like old-man blood vessels, clumsily pumping life in and out of the loop at the city's heart.

Richard's ride downtown that morning was more depressing than usual, meaning it was basically soul crushing. The day dawned especially cold, and Richard's particular train car didn't have heat—something not unusual, though this didn't make it any less terrible. The temperature on his phone read a crisp thirty-nine degrees, *inside* the train. The cold worsened his hangover. Every slight bump of the train racked his skull like an artillery explosion. The ride was one long, torturous barrage. Midway through, Richard nodded off, or fainted, only to be awakened by a man in a suit talking enthusiastically and obnoxiously on his phone about how he would project-manage the fuck out of that project. When a massively pregnant woman saw Richard wake, she pointed to her belly and asked for his seat. Richard lied and said he'd sprained an ankle, so couldn't stand. No one on the train offered the woman a seat.

As Richard rose to exit the train, feigning a limp, he noticed for the first time some unusual graffiti written in large red characters on the ceiling of the train.

NEXT STOP AUSCHWITZ

Richard wondered how different the Brown Line really was from a Holocaust train. The Holocaust trains couldn't have been more crowded than the Brown Line. The Holocaust trains most likely smelled worse, but how much worse? The Brown Line, frequented by homeless riders, often stank of trash and shit. Definitely more dead people on a Holocaust train. But then, dead people *had* been found on the Brown Line. The Holocaust trains must have moved faster, considering they were newer than the Brown Line— it took Richard forty minutes to travel six sluggish miles. The passenger load on the Brown Line was miserable. Probably not quite as miserable as the Holocaust riders, but certainly each passenger was unhappy in his or her own way. Clearly more diversity on the Brown Line.

Richard concluded that the main differences between the trains were their speed, their passenger demographics, their passenger life expectancies, and their destinations.

***

It was an ordinarily wretched day at the office. In the morning, Richard prepared for an important afternoon sales meeting with a prospect of his, Goldman Sachs. The deal with Goldman was a *big* deal. In the meeting, he would recommend a reduction in units through an investment in technology, which would lead to greater overall profitability, accountability, and of course flexibility. Should Goldman object, he would pull other abilities out of his ass. The reduction in units was key. That meant the elimination of employees, of cost. Profitability! Huge improvement in the bottom line. The head-count reduction alone would make the business case. Return on investment? Yes, sir, vice chairman, sir. Our preliminary, high-level study shows 375 percent, at least. That's a conservative estimate, by the way. *Hamiltonian* conservative. Goldman has low-hanging fruit everywhere. More figures to come in our deeper-dive analysis, set for the next phase. Don't forget adaptability. And *scalability*! Include terminal value and the tax component in our calculations and we can double that return on investment. Yes, double. Thanks, well, you've gotta think outside the box on this particular subject, vice chairman. Sign here. No, thank you. Looking forward to working with your team. In the meantime, may I suggest a drinkability? Did I say that? Haha hehe! Ha. Long week. Great, thanks again. You have a fine weekend as well. Weather looking brisk. All hands on deck next week! Great. Just great.

Throughout the meeting, fantasies of suicide played out in Richard's head. Luckily for him, the meeting ended early, and the day was nearly over. He was happy to see it was happy hour. Just in time. He could feel his fingers shaking and the delirium tremens coming on. Time for the Friday call to the wife, insinuating he would be home extremely late, if at all.

"Hi, honey. Yes I'll be home after I grab a drink or two at Stocks and Blondes no I won't be late I'll catch an early train home I promise oh and did I mention we can get that Downton Abbey kitchen you wanted no well we can get that kitchen it will look beautiful just like in that godforsaken show yes tell Andy I love him no I won't drink too much wait Andy did what in preschool fuck me we'll talk about it when I get home goodbye no I will not be late Jesus holy fucking Christ calm yourself woman I'll only have a couple drinks no late nights I won't be pissed as anything tonight but don't wait up I've been working all goddamn week I'm thirsty as Moses wandering the Sahara fucking desert yes you heard me.

"Sahara. Fucking. Desert."

Let the night's adventure begin!

Richard planned to walk from his office in the financial district across the river to catch a Red Line north to a bar, where he would get dangerously drunk. He'd then either take the train home or sleep with a certain intern, in which case he would cab home at an extremely late hour. He'd rather not return home in the event he slept with the intern, but lately he'd been on the thinnest of ice with his wife. He worried his wife would suddenly leave him for her cardio-tennis instructor, or report him missing to the affluent police. The last time a Richard Lyons missing-person report was filed, the affluent police had suggested to his wife that he was cheating on her. Not good. The officer had said they got these calls from wives in the neighborhood all the time. "How dare they!" Richard gasped to his wife when he returned home the next morning, stinking a strange stink, like vodka perfume.

Richard set forth along the Michigan Avenue tourist route north across the river, observing his surroundings with an uncommon interest for someone so familiar with the city. He passed over the backward-flowing river, thinking to himself how peculiar a backward-flowing river was. He walked by a monument honoring the victims of the Battle of Fort Dearborn, then another, honoring victims of the Great Chicago Fire. Toward the lake, he saw the Navy Pier Ferris wheel circling in the last light of the setting sun. He tried to, but couldn't, remember the last time he'd ridden a Ferris wheel. A marquee advertised a Smashing Pumpkins concert at the Aragon Ballroom, then an agricultural-equipment trade show at McCormick Place. The agricultural show made Richard wonder when there had last been an actual, operational farm within city limits. Had to have been a hundred years. He was sure not to make eye contact with a homeless man collecting change within an empty bottle of limoncello. He did, for some reason, accept a green flyer advertising a show at the Green Mill Cocktail Lounge, from a girl in green. He started to sweat as he walked. The temperature had risen, unexpectedly, at least twenty degrees since the morning. His heavy coat was suffocating him.

Near his Red Line destination, Richard noticed with suicidal pleasure a "Caution: Falling Ice" sign. Hundreds of such signs littered the downtown from November to April, warning pedestrians of the potential for death-by-crushing. The signs were a huge middle finger from the property management companies to the rest of the world—an announcement from the mustache-twirling chief legal counsel, "We are not liable for your death by falling ice." Cue evil laugh.

Richard was attracted to the "Falling Ice" signs. He walked toward them, danced around them, smoked underneath them. They were like little holy shrines for him. Life insurance is tax-free, he thought. Kid doesn't need a father. I sure didn't. Then again, here I am standing in the middle of the city waiting to get crushed to death by falling ice. Touché. Lightning would be a more likely death. Will go out for a long walk during a thunderstorm in springtime. Write that down. With metal car keys in headband. Does life insurance cover suicides? Think so, but only after two years. When did I buy that policy?

Richard stopped by the "Falling Ice" sign. He looked up hopefully for a microwave-size iceberg, squinting at the rooftop's edge, but found none. Unfortunate. No reason to stay long. It was getting late, and he was thirsty. Golden Goldman victory hops awaited.

As he walked, he read three texts he'd received in a row from the friend he was to meet at the bar.

Wherefore art thou, King Richard?

The white queen is frisky

From the red whisky :)

The texts made Richard's heart jump. The white queen of course meant cocaine, and red whiskey meant red whiskey. Hurray! He hurried on until he saw another "Falling Ice" sign ahead in his path. Hurray again! Richard approached. There, leaning against the sign, was a tiny homeless girl, not three feet high, wearing a crown of gleaming red-leaf skeletons. She held a smaller cardboard sign, which read:

qarter for a farry tail

The girl had nothing with her but a plastic cup filled with change and a wooden pan flute. She looked familiar, but Richard couldn't place her. The familiarity was distant. He sensed he'd known the girl when he was a boy. He wondered how that could be possible, when she looked to be just a girl herself.

Richard was intrigued by the "Falling Ice" sign and by the strangely familiar fairy-tale salesgirl. He'd once liked a fairy tale. Hadn't he? Hard to remember that far back. He decided he'd pay for a fairy tale. As a bonus he might get crushed to death by falling ice while he waited under the sign, listening.

He put a ten-dollar bill into the girl's plastic-cup cash register.

The girl gave Richard a look of sarcastic surprise. Her eyes were intelligent and looked older than the rest of her. "Mister, ten whole dollars will buy you a different sort of fairy tale! For that much, if you like, I can make up a fairy tale of you, just for you. Would that suit you, mister?"

"The fairy tale of me? Ha! Have at it, by all means." Richard laughed, but it was a nervous laugh.

The girl started without so much as the bat of a lash over her revelator eyes.

A poor boy grew up and into a fine specimen of a businessman. One night, his wife said he would be pissed as lord off his fizzy cross of gold, and she was right, he would be pissed, even though he promised her he would not. The winter wind blew him home with the storm at some ungodly hour of the night, so drenched in Chanel No. 5 you would have guessed it was the flavor of the snow bucketing down. His wife went mad waiting for him. He'd crossed the line one time too many, she said to herself, but she'd said that many times before. Later that night, he snuck out of their bed, and his wife thought, sneaky devil, always sneaking around. His wife searched the house for him. She found him in his son's room. His wife couldn't imagine the boy ending up like his lying daddy, but he would. Squinting through the keyhole, she couldn't see anything until a white flash of winter lightning exposed them. Her husband was standing near the window with the boy's Spider-Man pajamas

*knotted about him like red ivy. The boy wore his
father's fancy necktie around his head like a crown.
They were playing and dancing. They giggled
together, "God save the bachelors, the bachelors of
finance. They've spent all their gold on golden
underpants." The two danced around the room, and
the wife wished to be with them. She walked in and
asked if she might share in the dance. The three
danced, one last dance.*

"That is your own personal fairy tale, mister. Thank you
kindly for your business."

Richard started sweating again, which was strange,
because he felt naked. He knew the story. The story was
most definitely his. It was a typical Friday night, maybe that
very Friday night. His head started to spin. He pissed his
pants a bit. He stood there, staring at the girl, as if he should
defend himself. But he couldn't think of any defense, so he
just stared, and as he stared, she emerged again as a memory
from his childhood.

"Thanks, uh, ah, eh … thanks." Richard stuttered
nervously. "You, um, look familiar. I, I … I think we've met?"

The girl stared back at Richard, turning her head
sideways in thought, as if she were trying to remember him.

"Maybe we have met. Did you ever believe in magic?"

He had.

As a boy, Richard had thought the city was made of magic.
The old-man magician had told him so. He'd believed that
mermaids swam within Buckingham Fountain. He'd

dreamed of water fairies dancing after dark on the backward-flowing river. He'd been scared of the spirits of old Fort Dearborn, who haunted the high-rises built on their graves. An oracle had seen into the future at the northwest corner of North and Western. Rich had ridden the L as if it were a dragon drenched in pixie dust, set to soar over the lake and along the coast. There'd been magic everywhere then.

But that was then, when he was a boy. As a man, spirits were drunk and not dreamed. He snorted pixie dust, and while it made him high, he could never truly fly. The only Oracle he knew was a software corporation he'd once consulted for. Dragon was a text-to-speech mobile assistant app. Mermaids were mythology. The city was all steel and asphalt. And magic was something only children believed in, not Richard.

Richard believed in nothing.

He looked to the sky, not for falling ice, but for the place the magic had been relegated. Dim shafts of red light glowed within the pillars of western horizon between the skyscrapers, reminding him the sun had set not long ago. The moon shone down from above white stars, which were indistinguishable from airplane headlights, twirling together above the afterglow. It was the moment between afternoon and evening when the moon and sun swapped ownership of the sky. Twilight.

"What *is* your name, girl?" Richard asked. "Will you at least tell me that much?"

"I'll tell you," she said, smiling, "but only if you perform a magic trick for me."

Magic trick. Right. Without thinking, Richard pulled a 24-karat-gold fountain pen from his jacket. The pen had once been sacred to Richard. It had been awarded to him when he was promoted to vice president of something by a senior vice president and group president. He usually kept it in a tiny frame in his office. How it had ended up in his jacket, he couldn't say. But he had to make magic with it.

Richard scribbled a large "M" on the "Falling Ice" sign. The sign now read:

Caution: Falling MIce

A bow from Richard and applause from the girl.

"You're mad as the old king. Yes, you are. Total madman!" the girl laughed, pleased at the trick.

Richard bowed again. "Now, live up to your end of the bargain. Tell me your name."

"It's Piper. But you wouldn't remember my name, would you? We've met once before, but that was when you were someone else entirely, and we were entirely somewhere else. And anyway, a dandelion is a pretty flower to a boy, but no more than a pesky weed to a man. Your life and everything in it, even this city, it's all become a tangled patch of weeds. Hasn't it?"

"Piper, Piper …" Richard whispered under his breath. He was getting close.

The girl looked up at him, eyebrows raised, guessing his thoughts. "Tell you what. Throw that stupid-ass golden pen into the river as far as you can, and if you throw it far enough,

I'll tell you exactly how it is you think you know me."

Fine. Richard took the golden pen from his pocket, crow-hopped, and flung it into the far depths of the river like a champion golden-pen javelinist. Problem was, it had been such a long time since he'd crow-hopped. He'd lost all his crow-hopping ability. His weak knees buckled under his fat beer belly. He fell squarely onto his back, striking his head against the sharp edge of a sewer cap.

As Richard lay on the sidewalk in a daze, the mechanical clatter of the city quieted, and he heard only a whistle from the little girl's flute. She played him a familiar song, one of those songs that carries with it the remembrance of some great event. The song penetrated a dark, hidden corner of Richard's mind like a light from the past, helping him to remember. Richard opened his eyes and stared up from the ground at the twilight. He saw a girl in a white dress sailing through the sky. It was the same girl he'd seen during that college adventure, soaring among the dark funnel clouds, her blonde hair like the tail of a kite.

He remembered. She was a character within a boyish adventure he'd had long ago, a different adventure than the sort he'd grown accustomed to. It had been the most peculiar adventure, with kings, queens, ghosts, cowboys, Indians, elves, more. And there had been a girl.

No, not the flying girl. Another girl.

Richard closed his eyes again as he lay on the sidewalk. The lovely song tingled his ears. And as it played, he remembered all he'd forgotten.

II

"I had this dream. We danced a dance,
even the fairy, who crawled up my pants."

Fairy of the Tale

Ghost in the Graveyard

Richard remembered the time he was Rich.

Rich, as in the name. He'd been called that as a boy. Rich the boy had been long forgotten by Richard the man, the memory of his younger self erased one night after one too many vodka tonics.

Richard was much different from the boy Rich. Maybe Rich hadn't been as savvy as Richard now was when it came to the arts of commerce and capitalism, but Rich had possessed many of the virtues Richard had no use for as the vice president of something. Rich had been honest, sincere, generous, compassionate, brave. Rich had also been younger, and younger is better than older. What's more, Rich had played games. He'd loved games.

Here was Rich one night toward the end of boyhood, sometime between the last game of kick the can and the first can of beer: He had reached that proud point when a child can outlast his parents into the night, an important milestone in the lives of all concerned. His mother was sound asleep, his father ashes in a river. The night was his. What to do with it?

He'd play a game, of course. Ghost in the graveyard.

For those unfortunates who've never played ghost in the graveyard, here's a primer: It's a form of tag, or hide-and-seek. The player designated ghost must pursue all non-ghosts. The non-ghosts caught by the ghost become ghosts themselves, and aid in the capture/possession of the remaining non-ghosts. The game is rarely played in an actual graveyard, because that would be creepy. (Also, trespassing.) Cemetery play carries with it the risk of encountering actual ghosts, too, which would confuse things. So the game is ordinarily played in the parks of the city at sunset, usually on a Friday night.

The game of ghost in the graveyard we're concerned with—the one involving Rich, on that long-ago night—happened in autumn, when the wind blew its hardest, separating all the dying leaves from the trees and scattering them on the ground in globs of red and yellow. The game was held within a great city park. It might have been Portage Park, Wicker Park, Morgan Park, Lincoln Park, or Albany Park. All we know is it was played in a great park, dotted with dead globs of leaves from the drowsy trees. Lights from apartments, the shops beneath them, and street lights shone down upon the playing grounds, in accordance with the natural law of the city, which states it must never get truly dark.

The game Rich played that night would go down in history as legendary, easily the most acclaimed of his generation. Because the girl was finally caught. She had supposedly never been caught, not even when older teenagers deigned to play the game. In fact, she was thought so uncatchable, it was rare that anyone chased her. Rumor had it that a boy once ran so fast trying to catch her, he outran his own shadow, and had to stop and wait for the shadow to catch up. By the time it did, the girl was long gone. Because of her reputation, the only occasion anyone had chased her was when they didn't know her.

Rich didn't know her.

***

Rich started the game as the ghost. She may have been ghostly, but he was definitely the ghost, at least for the purposes of the game. Rich would rather not have been the ghost, but he was new to that particular city park, and being the new player, he had no choice. You see, the measure of a boy, just before he becomes a man, is based mostly on how fast he can run. Rich had to be evaluated by the other players.

Rich started the game in dominating fashion, as he normally did. He didn't look it, but he was a fast runner. He took pride in his ability to run. His father once told him he'd inherited his athletic ability from a distant relative named George Gipp, aka "the Gipper." The Gipper is recognized as one of the greatest collegiate football players from the leatherhead era of the early 20th century. Rich never really knew if the relation his father claimed was true, but he liked to believe it was.

Rich picked off most of the slower players within the first few minutes of the game. He was making excellent progress in his term as ghost. And then he saw her. She appeared out of thin air, as she had a tendency to do. She approached Rich mostly out of boredom, and became all the more bored at the sight of him, at least initially. Rich was a boring five-foot-nothing with a boring brown crew cut and only slightly interesting freckles dotting a round face that could only be described as boring. But, as uninteresting as he was to look at, she found herself walking toward him, as if he had something, something she couldn't see from far away.

That was how Rich first saw her, coming too near to him, daring him to chase her. And she looked worth chasing. She looked different. Her eyes were not the color of eyes, and her hair was not the color of hair—each was kaleidoscopic, changing slightly as she moved, so that it was hard for him to tell the exact color. He decided on a powder blue. She was dressed fashionably, grungily, in torn-up blue jeans and a plain white T-shirt. Beneath the whimsical park shadows, her age was anyone's guess. One second she was a woman, the next a little girl, then a woman again. She finally settled somewhere in between, at about Rich's age.

Rich was surprised by the new girl. Where had she come from? He hadn't seen her when the game started. He would've noticed a girl like her. She had to have been a fast runner to come so close to him, *the* ghost. That, or stupid.

She wasn't exactly a runner, though she could run very fast when she felt like it. The rest of the park knew the sight of her, but only the sight of her. No one knew where she'd come from, where she was going, or what her name was. Once in a while, she just showed up to the games. She played but was never caught. She was too fast to be caught. The general sense among the players was that she went to a private school designated for blue-haired girls of excessive speed and mysteriousness.

She walked closer and closer to Rich, then closer still. She was taunting him. Rich couldn't believe it. If she was just going to stand there, so close, what choice did he have but to chase her? He feinted toward her. She didn't flinch. She didn't seem scared by him, or by anyone else. In fact, she was simply curious. To her, Rich was a plaything. She walked closer, inviting him to chase her and race her, inviting him to play. Then, she winked at him.

The wink was the last straw. Rich sprung at her, almost closing the space between them before she could react with a step in the opposite direction. In those first few seconds, she barely escaped him. That was how it all began.

Everyone stopped to watch the chase. The other players stopped playing to observe. Shopkeepers peered out windows, families looked down from their apartments, pedestrians stopped along the sidewalk, and cars braked in the middle of the surrounding streets. The wind stopped. It was as though time had stopped, and for a while it really had—a nearby clock tower became distracted by the race and stopped ticking.

After Rich missed her by mere fingertips, she pulled away from him, establishing a comfortable lead. Rich couldn't get anywhere near her now. She was too quick. He chased her in hopeless, embarrassing circles around and around the park. He was discouraged, but not defeated. So he kept chasing.

After a while longer, it became obvious to Rich that he couldn't beat her in a short sprint. But he thought if he was persistent, he might outlast her. In the city, no field extends for more than a block or two, so the Darwinian forces affect only powerful sprinters. Rich figured this girl, whoever she was, would eventually burn out—ideally, just before him.

The seconds before she slowed were long and tiring for Rich, but finally she did begin to slow, allowing Rich to catch up. By that time, the area around the field was dense with spectators. Rich tried to tag her, but when he reached out his arm, he slowed ever so slightly enough to allow her the few precious steps she needed to separate herself from him. This happened a few times, before he tried a full-on tackle from behind. This was his last chance to catch her, he knew, because he was completely exhausted.

The crowd gasped as Rich closed his eyes and leaped through the air toward her, drawing on his last speck of energy. He landed squarely on her back, his arms wrapped tightly around her, driving her forward with almost no effort at all. No effort was needed. The girl felt light as a cobweb.

He had caught her.

In the moment between Rich's first touch and their tumble through the leaves, something strange happened, like an unexpected daydream. In the dream, it seemed to Rich as if he were a rocket man, jetting with the girl into the ether, up through purple clouds, straight toward the moon. Like everyone else at the park, the moon had a surprised look on its face. The surrounding stars and planets had equally surprised looks on their faces. When Rich saw them all staring at him, he couldn't help laughing, and the second he did, the whole galaxy joined him, erupting in hysterical, deafening laughter. The girl beside him laughed loudest of all, and the sound of her laughter made Rich's blood buzz like he was high, which of course he was—he was flying higher and higher. The moon grew larger and brighter the closer they flew toward it. Soon everything was the yellow of the moon. It was so bright, Rich couldn't help shutting his eyes.

When he opened them, the girl's face was where the moon's had been. How she had gotten on top of him he couldn't say, but there she was, straddling him, staring down. She looked as surprised as the moon and stars, but also curious. Rich was more than curious. He'd never had a girl straddle him before. The closest contact he'd had with a girl his age was during a forced square dance lesson in the school gymnasium, to the fiddles of *Dixieland Delight*. He'd hated it. This, he loved. Of course, he was fairly well in love with the girl by this point in the story. The matter was settled with one view of her beautifully puzzled face framed against the glowing tips of the city skyscrapers off in the distance.

The two sat, huffing and puffing, looking at each other, waiting for something to happen. Rich was too tired and pleased to do anything. He'd caught her, and was in no rush. He could have lain there all night.

After he'd caught his breath, Rich decided to introduce himself.

"I'm Rich. What's your name?"

"I'm the Ghost in the Graveyard, now aren't I?"

She was.

And the embers never fade in your city by the lake,
the place where you were born

The True Source of the Great Chicago Fire, by Finbar Finnegan

Before she was a ghost, she was Francesca Finnegan. And when she came into the world, there was nothing so unusual as a name like Finnegan behind (or in front of) a name like Francesca. Those sorts of names were as rare as red diamonds, and there is nothing as rare as a red diamond. You might have heard one existed, but you never actually saw it. In that way, the name Francesca Finnegan suited her well.

She was rare.

Francesca's beginnings were tied to the three notorious days in the autumn of 1871 when the Great Chicago Fire raged. As the fire neared Holy Family Church, the head pastor, Father Patrick Hughes, pledged in prayer that if Holy Family were spared, he would create a shrine to Our Lady of Perpetual Help. At the shrine, he would place a candle for each victim of the fire, and those candles would burn forever.

Father Hughes's prayer was answered. The winds shifted, and as the rest of the city burned down, Holy Family sat peacefully unscathed. Father Hughes made good on his promise. To this day, the candles representing the victims of the fire are lit continuously (by electricity) in the church's east transept.

But there was always one candle missing. The candle rested right under the church's nose, entombed beneath the floor of the confessional. During a replacement of the church flooring, they found him there. His name was Finbar Finnegan. His remains lay in a shoddy ashwood box, not six feet deep in the ground. He carried with him a letter and a small baptismal candle.

The candle was the true source of the Great Chicago Fire, according to Finbar Finnegan.

The letter was the only known record showing that our Francesca Finnegan ever existed.

***

Dear Francesca,

As you read this, I am seated with the Holy Spirit somewhere in the clouds, undoubtedly south beyond the pale, finally relieved of our long, treacherous plight, and also of your sawney mother, who was like Medusa to me, turning my heart to stone. In a way, I am glad to be dying now on my own terms. Your mother would have found and murdered me soon I think. You were begot from a godless, debauched hoor, pardon me for saying it.

This letter will have been delivered to you by the Chinaman butcher called Chen. God bless the heart of every ungodly Chinaman, I swear on your grandmother's grave in Banbridge, there is no shrewder race of human I ever encountered, and if China can go on breeding Chens, we will all be Chinese someday. I considered seeking your uncle and giving him this letter for safekeeping, but he is a moonbat, and would surely forget to deliver it. He and your mother's clan have been a fellowship of birdbrains since before the discovery of cabbage. Do not mistake the stone structure on their family crest for some ancient castle dwelling. It is no castle at all. It is an immense lunatic asylum.

I write this letter with the one hand that isn't burned blacker than Judas in hell by that conflagration that overtook this fine city on the lake, during these few days in October. I lie in Holy Family Church, wholly fagged out. This place was spared, but is now filled with charred Catholics such as myself and Lester Lyons the lamplighter, lying not far from me. God take him, he looks like he was roasted well done over a spit. He is blacker than the banshees haunting the Ballingarry coal mines.

My heart has fewer beats left than would be required to record in the fullest of detail how I am found lying here dying, with no company but Chinaman Chen. I at least must relate to you how this grand blaze began, and my courageous role within the tale, setting the story straight before I breathe my last. No one else is left to tell the story.

***

The eighth of October began as an ordinary night by all accounts, with the exception of the unruly wind (one of those cutting winds from over the lake). These were gales meant for the tips of the tallest trees and mountains that touch the stars, not for some jackeen standing on the ground to withstand. I was happy as a Larry observing from my flat window as folks blew about in it as freely as the autumn leaves.

That evening, we finally held your baptism here in this church, not far from where I now die. You were the oldest child, I think, that was ever baptized in the history of baptisms. When I confessed to Priest Hughes you were already four years old, he was incensed, and demanded to know why I was so overdue in that most critical of Catholic rituals.

"Finbar, what in society have you been doing the past four years that you have not had the wherewithal to get little Francesca christened until now?"

"My sincere apologies, Father. You see, my wife, whom I firmly believe to be a disciple of Lucifer, abandoned Francesca and me for a career as a ringmaster and slut in a traveling gypsy circus. She left us starving victims of the potato blight early on. And then of course passage across the Atlantic and the hazardous journey west in a rickety wagon held together by spit and a prayer, and so on, and so on."

That testimony, all true as tea, mind you, backed Father Hughes off well enough.

At the baptism ceremony, I was awarded what the church calls a 'baptismal candle' on your behalf. I did not at the time suspect that this candle would be the source of the greatest catastrophe this city has known. How could I? I was never a prouder man in my history, and standing there with that candle lit, I probably looked hypnotized. Your skin shone as brightly as bass scales in that water, your hair a bluer blue than the clear sky, your whole self a sight of wonder to all in attendance.

After the baptism, I dropped off your newly baptized self at the house of a waged child watcher, then strolled over to Hanley's for a libation with your cousin Davey and Sergio the butcher. Alcohol was like the plague to Davey and many on that side of our family, but I thought the celebration warranted, given the respite of your soul from purgatory.

Davey was foostering about Hanley's that night, pissed blacker than the North Sea under a new moon, and that is black, blacker than Zulu tits, pardon me for saying it. He was rambling about his no-good wife, though I will not fault him for that, she is the same class of human as your sinful mother. I guess them to be third cousins, at least. Needless to say, Davey was on the lash. Hanley's was roaring with every cock of the walk at the ready to commit every sin in existence and to create new ones. A misadventure was in the cards.

"Red sky at night, my wife left me for a banker named Dwight, red sky in the morning ... red sky in the morning ... she is a spawn of Satan," rambled Davey.

"Davey, I believe the proper saying is, red sky at night, sailor's delight, red sky in the morning, sailor take warning," I noted. "And I may say the sky tonight is redder than the blood in your own veins, thinner than my baptized baby girl's lips it may be. A fine omen from the heavens on her baptism!"

"Davey, this weather is uncommon," Sergio explained. "There is an irregular wind blowing hard from the east."

"Shut it!" Davey roared. "I swear on King James's Bible you would not know a proper wind were it to blow the olive skin off your greasy Latin body straight into Lake Michigan. The wind is most certainly blowing in hard from the north."

"Calm yourself, Davey," I said. "You are both misinterpreting the course of the breath of God on this day. It is swooping down like an unseen eagle across the Great Plains from those Rocky Mountains in the west. It feels like a rhythm from home for me."

"If it's so rhythmic, Finbar, why don't you piss off out front, and while you're pissing, procure a bit of spare change for my rent that is now two months past due."

"Spare us your misfit ramblings, Davey. Sergio, how is business?"

Sergio loved to discuss the business of meat.

"The Greeks are making me a rich man with their cravings for red meat. Yesterday my daily shipment did not arrive, so I ground up cow eyeballs with pigs' feet, called it meatloaf, and was cleaned out by the time the church bells rang in the afternoon! The Chinese butcher Chen begs for my recipe, but I will not tell him. He'd blind every cow from here to Boston."

We went on fussing like that for the next few hours. Davey drank a considerable volume of wine, which in hindsight was especially odd, as he could not tell a cup of cold piss from a decent white. It shames me to admit I did not stop him from drinking at least five bottles of some newly shipped Catalonian stuff Hanley had supplied him. I assumed it was watered down. Hanley was a fiend in this and many other ways, a dishonest fellow by nature. Be that as it may, I find Davey less tolerable sober than I find your devil-worshiping mother generally, and that is saying quite a lot, so I did not mind that he was drinking himself into an early grave.

As Davey staggered out of the jacks toward the exit, utterly bolloxed, a pity for him exploded like a fireball inside my heart. I had suspected for some weeks that he had been evicted from his shanty on Rush Street, and felt the need to confirm the suspicion, or at least to follow the blackguard out, to ensure he found his way. So I followed him out the door, with that piteous flame in my heart destined to grow into a firedrake.

The sun did not sustain the revelry at Hanley's, and a moonless night draped the sky pitch. I did not have my own lantern handy, as I did not anticipate staying at Hanley's long. So, God forgive me, I supposed I could use your baptismal candle to light the night. Hanley kindly supplied me with a small holder for the candle, which I lit and carried with me as I left. This helped guide me after Davey.

The city night was not just black, it was wraithlike. The lamplights were all blown out on account of the extraordinarily severe crosswinds. I swear these gusts hit harder than any pugilist I ever saw, with the possible exception of your great-grandfather Brend the Bricklayer. When I was just a lad, not much bigger than you are now, I witnessed Brend leather the head clean off a Protestant's body, as easy as if he were cleaning dishes. That is what this wind was like.

Davey also had himself a lantern. He was doing his best not to drop it as he zigzagged left and right like some bit of mosquito blowing back and forth at the whim of the wind. I patiently mirrored his drunken dance, until we arrived at the intersection of LaSalle and Erie, at which point I overtook him. His lantern had been quenched by the winds in that intersection, so I relit it for him, with your little candle.

"Hohohoho, Mister Finnagain, you're going to be Saint Finnagain! Comeday morm and O, you're vine! Sendday's eve an, ah, you're vinegar! Hahahaha, Saint Funn, you're going to be fined again! Wake up, Finnagain Wake!" was all he rambled. It was his final declaration.

At the intersection, a curious scene was unfolding before our eyes. I will not forget the grave moments that followed, they are eternally branded in my mind. I can see them as well as Chen by my side now. The street was invaded by dust and legions of leaves sailing like locusts on the shoulders of that powerful wind. Within the leafy maelstrom, the pugnacious Karlovitz twins stood some ten paces from each other. Both looked totally ossified, waving pepper-box pistols and wildly screaming what I suppose were grave insults in their native Hun tongue. I think those two were the direct descendants of the barbarians that sacked Rome, absolute savages they were.

Now, the Karlovitz twins' loudly cursing or even physically attacking each other on any given day was about as common as your witchy mother's spending all my hard-earned wages on some luxurious gift for herself. That is to say, it happened with frequency. But, as often as the two Karlovitz twins fought, I had not ever seen each twin armed with a deadly weapon, and, as you may expect, the heart in my chest was crossways.

As I formulated an appropriate strategy for diminishing the ruckus, Davey foolishly engaged himself in the conflict. He wobbled over to one of the twins, the one called Joseph, I think. Drunk Davey grabbed Joseph Karlovitz by the collar and proceeded to deliver an awkward hug as only a truly langered man is capable of. As was often the case in his life, his timing was not good. Explosive gunfire abruptly silenced the music of the wind. Davey wailed. The bullet, or bullets, appeared to have struck him in the torso. He was all red, as if a vat of spaghetti sauce had spilled on him at supper.

Davey still had the lantern in his hand, even after he was shot and bleeding like Jesus on the cross. He staggered with it against the wall of a highly combustible underwear factory, where he sat exhaustedly against an errant haystack. I thought he would spend his dying last seconds there. I was only partially right.

In the meantime, the Karlovitz twins, realizing their folly at having shot drunk Davey, flagged down a horse and carriage. I suppose they meant for the vehicle to transport poor Davey to the doctor, but the lead horse had other plans. She completed a wide circle in the street, and in the process trampled the unshot portion of poor Davey, laying waste to his already banjaxed body. The owner of the horse scurried away south down LaSalle, likely fearing he might be prosecuted for murdering an Irishman, although Lord knows a dying rat in the street would get as much attention from the sheriff in most parts of this city.

Before I go on, recall Davey's lantern—that lantern lit from your own baptismal candle. Even after his trampling, the candle remained miraculously unbroken and glowing at Davey's side.

It was no smaller miracle for Jesus to be resurrected on Easter than it was for Davey to still be alive, and alive he was. I swear on the infinite virginity of the Blessed Virgin Mary, he stood up on his own two feet looking redder than the sunset on Galway Bay. The bloody cunt, pardon me for saying it, picked up his lantern and started strolling down the street. Had he not been soaked in his own blood, you might have guessed he had just woken from a pleasant nap.

He would not get far.

At that odd hour of the night, Catherine O'Leary was guiding an old, blind cow down the street. When I saw her and that cow, I remember thinking three things: First, why in God's grace is Catherine O'Leary walking down the middle of the street with a cow at this hour? Second, why does the aforementioned cow appear older than Adam and have no eyeballs? And last, this is the strangest evening I've had since my cousin Barry the Blind married a man beneath a harvest moon in the woods of Balleycastle. I wonder as I write this if Sergio that scurvy Roman is not baking meatloaf with that cow's eyeballs!

At the fateful intersection of LaSalle and Huron, Davey tipped his scrounge hat, dripping with blood, to Catherine, and proceeded to pet the old blind beast, as a child might pet a small dog. Catherine was of course speechless as the Ghost of Christmas Yet to Come. The cow was not accustomed to being petted by Davey, and did not like it. She reared her hindquarters and, with an extraordinary display of agility, punted Davey squarely in his mouth, straight through the gates of heaven or (more likely) hell, and also through a window of the underwear factory, with the force of cannon fire. The hangman's knot could not have given him a faster death.

When Mary's cow horseshoed Davey's carcass through the window, he somehow kept a grip on his lantern (the one lit from your baptismal candle), and was therefore joined with it in the building, which promptly caught fire.

I presume it was the lantern fire's coming into contact with a pile of oily underwear, or some other highly combustible item blessed by Satan, which caused the factory to catch fire, but I can't say with certainty what it was. All I can say is that the building was transformed into a blast furnace faster than your harpy mother could slap me in the face, and you are too young to remember how fast that could happen. I might have been slapped five times before breakfast for no other reason than that it was not breakfast yet.

From the underwear factory, the fire spread with unchecked sway like typhus in the arms of the wind. The city was burning hot as Rome under the torches of Nero, quick as you read this, all of it having originated from your own baptismal candle.

***

I have not the strength to relay in full detail how I heroically, but unsuccessfully, endeavored to retrieve the body of Davey from that inferno, or how I made my way to the orphanage on Kinzie, where I probably saved a dozen bastards with half my body burned off, or how I clambered twelve stories up the side of old General Grady's textile factory to retrieve a basket of tomcat kittens from a man burned blacker than your mother's soul. From that height, the lake looked like a flowing quagmire of molten gold under the shadow of the fire. I don't doubt you will hear all these tales in due time within the local periodicals, and I will be proclaimed a heroic saint of sorts, in agreement with Davey's final drunken declaration.

I am hearing it told among some of those here in this church that Catherine O'Leary's cow kicked over a lantern in a barn, and that this was the root of the blaze.[3] As you now know this is not the true tale, but let the ignorant masses blame the cow. I do not wish for the tale I have told you to be distributed to the general public. I doubt that Davey wants to be immortalized as the founder of the fire, or that you would like for it to be generally known that your own baptismal candle was the fire's true source.

Baptismal candles are not meant to burn down cities.

***

The fire that burned this city down is a damp coal compared with the flames ignited within me by that spark in your eyes on the day you were born. When the soggy roots of trees have penetrated my dead bones

---

[3] *O'Leary was likely blamed for the fire because she was an Irish Catholic, despised by many. Funny how an Irish Catholic was indeed responsible for drunkenly burning down the entire city. All this time we just had the wrong one.*

underneath the ground, that spark will still shine within me.

My last link to you in this life is this little baptismal candle. The light from this candle has begun your story, and closed the final chapter in the story of a city that you will never know.

I can hear the rain lashing off the roof now. Probably only a few embers left, fading like me. May they temper your heart into soft steel, wherever your heart is now …

I am sapped as a maple.

Your Dying Father,
Finbar Finnegan

Postscript

One more thing before I am fully dead.

I spent a disproportionate amount of wages on books for you. Truly, we were at times nearly starved by little children's books. You would never allow me to put you down for the night with just one measly story having been told, so here is another for you, one you cannot buy from any bookshop.

I fear you will not learn our native language, though I am not sure how much good it would do you anyway in this city. In that language, the phrase "Tír na nÓg" means "Land of the Young" or "Land Under the Water." In our folklore, it is another world said to exist somewhere inaccessible to those without invitation from a fairy maiden. The entrance to Tír na nÓg is under the water or across the sea. This is a tale about a regular old Irish potato such as myself who once visited Tír na nÓg.

It goes like this.

One of the fairy maidens of Tír na nÓg fell in love with a run-of-the-mill Irish potato such as myself. Lucky guy, you'd think, and for a while he was. The fairy maiden swept him off his muddy feet to Tír na nÓg, on a magical horse that could travel under the water. Tír na nÓg turned out to be quite the holiday spot, where all was forever young and mystical and beautiful and musical. The man loved the fairy maiden and all else within the magical realm. Time did not exist in Tír na nÓg, and so the man spent a hundred years there without aging a day. After spending all that time there, the man eventually became homesick and declared he must return home. The fairy maiden warned him that if he were to leave, he would regret it, that he would grow old as a pearl mussel once he set foot on the ground outside Tír na nÓg, that all the years would catch up with him. The man, being of the stubborn sort, did not heed her fairy warning, and so rode the magic horse home. Sure enough, when he stepped off the horse and touched the ground, a hundred years passed through him in an instant. The man found he had become elderly and quickly died of old age.

The end.

Now that I think of it, you have the look of a fairy maiden ...

Mr. Cat the cat conductor poses with timepiece

The Lavender Line

"What's your favorite color?"

Francesca asked Rich the all-important color question after she'd introduced herself and they'd risen from the leafy park grounds. The color question was Francesca's favorite, along with, "Can you play?" Richard the hops-drinking vice president of something preferred, "What do you do?" or, "Where do you golf?" Sadly, this was the second-to-last time Rich would answer the color question, and so marked the beginning of the end for him. Once people stop asking you what your favorite color is, you're done for.

Rich decided then and there his favorite color was something like her hair. "Blue," he said. "You?"

"Red. Reminds me of my red friend, the esteemed Mr. Fox, of the Red Line." Rich wasn't sure who or what she meant by her red friend, the esteemed Mr. Fox, of the Red Line, but decided against any questioning on the subject. She might think it rude, or stupid—he wasn't exactly sure what the word "esteemed" meant.

"Let's see, blue and red, red and blue, blue and red," Francesca thought aloud. "Mix those two, add a dash of stardust, and we have a lavender. That's settled, tonight we'll go for a Lavender Line ride."

Here, Rich felt he should correct her. She could talk about esteemed foxes all she wanted, but when it came to city trains, he was the expert. His uncle was employed by the Chicago Transportation Authority in an important office job, and had educated him in all there was to know about city transportation. Rich was sure there was no Lavender Line. There were the Red, Orange, Purple, Green, Blue, Pink, and Yellow lines. Definitely no Lavender in there. Maybe she'd meant Purple.

"Francesca."

"Yes?"

"There is no Lavender Line. Did you mean the Purple Line?"

"Nope, meant what I said. Lavender, like salamander. The Lavender is something different from the other trains. It's not like the ones you ride. It's bigger. It's faster. It's the most entertaining of all city trains."

Rich still didn't believe her. "What direction does the Lavender Line run? What neighborhoods does it pass through? I've got a map of all the CTA train routes in my bedroom, and I've never seen a Lavender Line. Not once. Never heard of it, either."

"It's on the map, just not your map. It runs east down Western, south down North, on through Lakeview to Riverview, then back all the way to 1802. It generally runs through the East Side of the city."

You can imagine the confused look on Rich's face. For

Western Avenue runs north and south, and North Avenue runs east and west. That bit about Lakeview, Riverview, and 1802 made no sense to him at all, and the East Side comment was the craziest. Everyone knew there was no East Side to the city. The East Side was Lake Michigan.

Yet as delusional as Francesca sounded, Rich decided to follow her. He thought maybe she was just playing a game, and he liked games. He would play along.

"Fine, then. Lavender it is. Where do we catch this Lavender Line?"

"East Side, like I said. Not that you'd know where that is. If you've never heard of the Lavender Line, chances are you've never heard of the East Side. It's somewhere between Roseland and Graceland, not totally outside Chicagoland, well inside the hinterland. It's in the summertime, before the days have shortened and it's gotten the least bit cold. That's not to say you can't have a little snow here or there. You just have to ask the right people for it. It's a little different as far as the people go, but not so different from anywhere else you've never been."

That was how Francesca talked—all rhymes and riddles and gibberish. To Rich, most of it sounded like gibberish, and it very well may have been. Rich didn't doubt the possibility that some mysterious neighborhood existed beyond anywhere he'd ever heard of or visited. After all, Chicago was a city of neighborhoods, each with its own borders, like little vassal states, governed by the greater kingdom. It was the strange way she explained the East Side that made it hard to believe in.

Still, Rich wondered what the East Side might be like, if it existed. It sounded interesting, if it existed.

***

Rich followed Francesca away from the game of ghost in the graveyard and into the darkening city night. The two roamed a labyrinth of alleyways, gangways, and streets in such a weird, winding way, it wasn't long before Rich lost all sense of place and neighborhood and felt totally lost. Not that he minded being lost. He trusted Francesca. She had this air of confidence in the way she led him, and the way she walked, with this stately gravity, her shoulders hardly bouncing, as if she floated on air. You could see she wasn't lost.

After they turned onto a particularly desolate street, Francesca grabbed hold of Rich's hand and started running, and when she touched his hand, it felt like fireworks exploded in his head. As they ran up the street, the fireworks continued in him, under him, over him, and he couldn't hear anything above the explosions. He felt wobbly, held up by the grip of someone who he realized then was no ordinary girl, and if you saw them running you'd have thought from their smiles that it was the last day of school, let out minutes before.

They ran until they encountered the Lavender Line depot, in the middle of a small bridge overlooking a narrow, fast-flowing branch of the Chicago River. Rich did not yet know this was the Lavender Line depot. But in the center of the bridge, Francesca stopped and stood looking down over the railing, into the river. She stared and stared, as if searching for something precious she'd accidentally dropped. Rich looked down but saw nothing but dark water.

After a couple of minutes of staring into the river, Rich jokingly asked Francesca if there was a train in it.

"Yes," she said plainly. "Yes, as a matter of fact, there is."

An airplane flew low and loud over them, making a sharp descent westward, toward the airport. A line of plane lights trailed behind it in the sky over Lake Michigan, each following the same flight path. Rich looked up and saw how the lights of the planes dominated the city sky, outshining the stars. Another plane approached, and in the few short seconds it passed over their heads, several unexpected things happened.

First, Rich noticed a sparkle out of the corner of his eye, in the water. Looking over the railing, he saw a flurry of tiny lights, like swimming fireflies, just below the river's surface. It looked as if the lights from the plane reflecting on the water had broken into a hundred little pieces and gone swimming about in all directions. As he stared at the pieces, Francesca let go of his hand. She had to let it go, to dive off the bridge. She disappeared with hardly a splash under the water, among the lights. Rich's first reaction was to leap after her into the river without a thought, which he did, but in the seconds between when he left the ground and hit the water, he did have some thoughts. He wasn't scared of drowning, or of the impact. He was scared of whatever was in the water itself. He could hardly guess what all those lights were below the surface. He thought if there were undiscovered species anywhere, they'd be in the depths of the Chicago River.

Rich's eyes opened wide under the water, despite his best efforts to keep them closed. They opened at the shock of the cold, biting him from everywhere. He looked for Francesca, but she was nowhere to be found. All he saw, a few feet under him, was one of those specks of light glowing faintly, so he swam toward it. As he drew closer, he saw it was shaped like a fairy. The thing was no bigger than a perch, but with the face and shape of a girl, and little wings acting as fins on its back. It would allow Rich to get within arm's reach, then dart away, drawing him deeper and deeper, until he found himself at the bed of the river. There, standing on the muddy ground, out of breath, he was swarmed by an army of the glowing fairies. They pushed him down, down, down, until his knees buckled below him into the earth, then down farther. They pushed him down until the river was gone, and he felt as if he were falling through the air.

***

Rich didn't land. He simply stopped, finding himself only a little damp.

He stopped somewhere under the river, in the middle of a large, shadowy cavern, which looked something like an abandoned mine shaft. High wooden beams held up the earth above, and railroad tracks flowed in and out of huge black tunnels on opposing walls. The only light came from a handful of torches affixed to the walls' surfaces. Francesca stood beneath one of the torches. Rich was relieved to have found her again. He joined her and they waited side by his side under the torchlight, as if nothing out of the ordinary had happened, as if they were simply waiting for a train.

Which they were.

"This is the first stop of the Lavender Line," Francesca said, her voice echoing through the cavern. "I expect the train may or may not arrive now or later."

"What were those little lights in the water?" Rich asked.

"Who, the water sprites? You've never seen a water sprite? I suppose that's to be expected. They only come out at night, when a plane passes low. They mistake plane light for starlight. They used to love starlight. When there were still stars over the city, the water sprites would glow and sing and dance in the river from dusk till dawn. Not anymore. They come out less and less now that the stars have gone away."

"Oh. Dancing water sprites." This was all Rich could muster.

"Can you dance yourself?" Francesca asked.

"Oh, sure, yeah. Yeah, I dance. I dance all the time," Rich lied. He couldn't dance. Not a step. He'd tried it on a few occasions and had been thoroughly embarrassed, almost shocked at how horrendous a dancer he was.

"Excellent, then you'll be my date for the ball at the Aragon Castle tonight."

Before Rich could figure out whether he was pleasantly or disturbingly surprised at being declared Francesca's date to a castle ball, the noise of a fast-approaching train consumed the cavern. It wasn't the pathetic, drawling clankety-clank of the L. It was an explosive mechanical howl, followed by the drawn-out shriek of a whistle. Soon the Lavender Line, a hulking steam locomotive, beating sparks out of the rails it rode on, burst forth from a dark tunnel in a mass of steam and color. The train's exterior was a shiny metallic silver. The headlights beamed a powerful purple, shining like a black light throughout the cave. The effect made Francesca's blue hair turn invisible. Francesca noticed Rich staring at her and smiled. Her teeth glowed.

As soon as the train came to a stop, a conductor stepped out and paced the area near the train doors, looking at his watch, glancing here and there for passengers, doing the things conductors do. From a distance, Rich thought the conductor wore a massively thick orange beard on his face, but as they approached him to board the train, Rich saw he was mistaken. The conductor had no beard at all. He had orange fur, and it covered his face completely. To Rich's astonishment, the conductor had the head of a house cat! Rich tried not to stare but couldn't much help it.

The conductor roared an "All aboard!" sounding more wildcat than house cat.

Francesca grabbed Rich's hand and led him onto the Lavender Line. The passenger car they entered had two levels, above and below. A narrow walkway ran down the center, dividing two rows of double seats. The train-car arrangement was ordinary. The passengers were not.

The first passenger Rich saw had a huge fish head and body, but the legs of a woman, in black lace nylons, ending in feet wearing high heels. The fish-woman flipped through the pages of a newspaper, using her flippers. A giant

Minotaur occupied two seats, his legs crossed comfortably, tapping his horns against the window in a bored sort of way. A family of little gray goblins gazed out a window together, pointing at this or that thing excitedly, like sightseers on a family train trip through the city. A faun with reading glasses sipped a coffee nervously and shook his head, looking irritated with the goblin family next to him. A Cyclops stared at Rich out of his one huge eye, bobbing his head back and forth for apparently no reason. Through the center of the aisle limped a hunchback, peddling books from a cart.

Needless to say, Rich felt out of place.

The train lurched forward as soon as Francesca and Rich sat down, across from each other in a spot where two rows of seats faced each other. Francesca sat next to a tiny little dwarf-looking creature (actually an elf), who carried with him a crumpled brown paper bag almost twice his size. The little man looked like a garden gnome. He had a plump face covered with a white, curly beard, and wore a dingy Cubs hat. He was so small, Rich hadn't noticed him until after they'd sat down.

Francesca struck up a conversation.

"Who are you, little sir, and what is that in your brown bag?"

Little princess plays with dandelions in the middle of the Middle Ages

Templeton Goodfellow

I am a hero.

Name's Templeton Goodfellow, a fine fellow, secret inventor of limoncello. It was the Tuscan princess Maria de' Medici helped me form the lemony concoction. She had the most beautiful ghost that'll ever be, but if you're wanting to know what I got here in this brown bag, then her story is for a different time. In this bag, I got a fresh bottle of Jeppson's Malört. Let me tell you about me and Malört Swedish Liquor, and how Malört came to be flavored in the city above.

I know you don't know me. My brother Robin, on the other hand, you might. He goes by Puck, the smug fuck. Shakespeare quoted him in a midsummer's dream, "Thou speak'st aright; I am that merry wanderer of the night." Merry wanderer indeed! The merry asshole wandered into a mousetrap in the East End during the Great Plague of London. Since the accident, he's been paralyzed from the nipples down, bedridden at my auntie's flat in Stratford-upon-Avon.

I'm an elf, but not a normal elf, if there is such a thing.

What I mean is, I'm not like these frauds you see in the movies with their fine silver hair like harp string. As you can see, I'm five inches tall with ratty hair and skin that looks its age—roughly ten thousand years old. I've been jaundiced for most of the last century as a result of late-stage alcoholism, which is why my skin is the color of piss.

I deposit spirits in spirits for a day job. Let me explain how that works.

When any liquor is created for the first time, there's this one important step in the process you probably aren't aware of. The hidden step has to do with the deposit of a spirit, a soul, or a ghost into the liquor itself. After fermentation, it's my job to complete this step, by guiding (sometimes forcing) the chosen spirit into the alcohol. The spirit provides the real flavor.

The finest liquors hold the most beautiful souls. As I said, limoncello wouldn't exist without Maria de' Medici. Joan of Arc was responsible for Dom Ruinart champagne. The first true grappa was made with Caravaggio's spirit, after I encountered it, over-served to death on port wine in a port bar near Genoa.

As fine liquors tend to house beautiful souls, the most repulsive liquors cage reprehensible ones. Stroh's tastes like Adolf Eichmann's soul would, because his soul is the primary flavoring. You can thank Stalin for smoked salmon vodka. After Vlad Dracula was executed, I bound his ghost and deposited it into a jar of beet wine so rancid, it hasn't been tried for five hundred years.

Then, there's Malört.

Malört originally contained a serial rapist by the name of Nathan Schwartz. I changed old Nate out when Malört gained notoriety in Chicago. The Midwest never suited Nate anyway. I replaced him with a notorious dago, Alphonse Gabriel Capone. Capone was a rare case in that he forfeited his spirit before his eventual death. It happened on the night of the Saint Valentine's Day massacre, when Capone ordered the execution of nine rival gang members in a Lincoln Park alley.

On that night, Capone occupied his usual corner booth at his favorite speakeasy, the Green Mill Cocktail Lounge. Place is still there today, believe it or not, still filled with spirits. Capone sat fortuitously near me at the end of the bar. He was with a little lava-lamp-shaped Sicilian girl. I was stag, as I generally am, heavily drunk, as I generally am, listening to a jazz band play above the speakeasy whispers.

At the exact point in time when the Valentine's massacre was carried out, Capone's soul was expelled from his body, a natural consequence after such an evil act, and something not so uncommon as you might think. I see souls give way before the body every single day in this city. Acting on instinct, and taking advantage of my proximity to the demon spirit, I leapt from my stool and gave the thing a mighty thump on the skull, knocking its lights clear out. I forced it into the nearest bottle I could find, which happened to be Malört, and there the spirit of Capone swims forever, and you understand why Malört tastes so bitter.

I ended up drinking a bottle or so of Malört myself that night, mostly out of curiosity. Stuff turned out worse than I thought it would. Wouldn't mix with anything. My mouth reeked of something like dirty pennies in the days after. As I drank, I laughed at the irony of the situation, how the most successful bootlegger in history ended up a bootleg himself. Reminded me of the richest Roman, Marcus Crassus, getting molten gold poured down his throat by the Parthians. Try Steel Reserve, it has Crassus in it.

When I left the Green Mill that night, I strolled down Lawrence Avenue to the lakeshore as I tend to do when I get seriously drunk and depressed. I went to Montrose Beach, where there's an odd sand dune that never accumulates snow. Within that dune, I hide the finest limoncello, and with it the spirit of Maria de' Medici.

I dug up the bottle, opened it, and sang a song to Maria. It was a song she'd last heard centuries ago, when she first found me among the weeds, the little princess she was, blowing the bulbs off white dandelions for fun.

Frisk me, Maria
I've got sangria
Up the leg of me drawers

I heard her laugh within the bottle. She sounded like waves in a seashell.

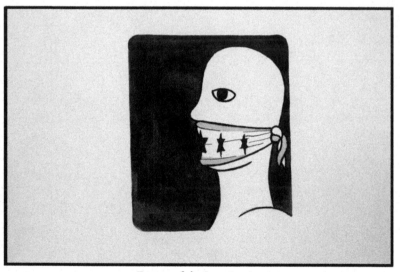

Enemy of the Imagination

A Roguish Coat of Arms

"Wait, wait," Francesca said to Templeton. "You said you were a hero. Why are you a hero?"

The tiny old elf took a deep breath and removed the bottle of Malört from his brown paper bag. "My hero story is in that story of Maria, and, like I said, that story is for another time. Come, have a taste of some sweet Malört with me." As Templeton said this, he winked deviously at Rich, as if sharing some heinous secret.

Rich hadn't tasted a true hard liquor at that point in his life. The only thing he'd ever drunk with alcohol in it was an alcopop called Hooch. Hooch looked and tasted like lemonade. In fact, you'd probably prefer it to lemonade. It's sweeter. Malört is in a different class of spirit entirely—the worst class. The first taste of hard liquor is hard enough when it's anything else. The first taste of Malört can be a traumatic experience for even the most seasoned drinker.

Rich had heard Templeton's description of Malört, so of course he wanted nothing to do with it. He knew he wasn't ready. The problem, though, was Francesca. Rich guessed she would taste it. If Francesca would try it, how could he refuse? He had no choice.

Templeton handed Rich the bottle. "I have a cold, so be sure to wipe the mouth. Jerking off with a cold is like reading a book upside down. You can start, but never finish, and there is no satisfaction in the endeavor."

Rich looked at the bottle. The color of the liquor reminded Rich of piss, and if there was a blind taste test, piss would easily win over Malört, unless the person pissing had been drinking Malört, in which case there would be a tie. The bottle label was marked with an interesting heraldic crest. The crest had the silhouette of a man's face, his mouth bound shut with the city flag. Rich stared at the design, wondering what it represented. He'd never seen anything like it.

When Rich looked up from the bottle, he saw the faces of Templeton, Francesca, and everyone else on the train staring at him, waiting for him to take a sip. The conductor had even stopped in the aisle and was glaring at him with cunning cat eyes. The train was noiseless. Rich felt like he was at the center of some initiation ritual, and worried that if he didn't try the drink, he'd be thrown off the train. So he shut his eyes tightly and did what had to be done.

The smell of the bottle burned a warning through Rich's nose before anything else, and when the liquor first met his tongue, he thought, "This is poison," and believed he would be poisoned to death by a tiny elf. The taste was such a shock to his senses, it caused his whole body to convulse. He jerked his shoulders forward, as if he'd been kicked in the stomach.

His throat let out a guttural screech he thought was his own death rattle, until he didn't die. The Malört swam down his throat and into his stomach like burning gas, scalding everything it touched on the way down. The Malört's vile essence stuck in his mouth like peanut butter. It caused his face to twist and turn as if he were possessed. Then, he opened his eyes.

He'd done it!

A chorus of laughter, applause, and praise erupted. Several passengers actually stood up and bowed to Rich. The fish-woman shook his hand with her fin. The conductor walked by him clapping, a mischievous smile on his feline face. Rich forced a smile through his own clenched teeth and watering eyes. He swore in that moment he would never drink Malört again, but he *had* done it, and the taste of victory was disgusting.

Now it was Francesca's turn. Rich tried to hand the bottle to her, but she raised her palms in defense and said plainly, "You'll suck my dick before I have so much as a sniff of *that!*"

Rich reflexively pulled the bottle back to his chest, looking at Francesca with the most perplexed stare, unsure of how he felt at the thought of sucking a girl's dick, and how strange it sounded for a girl to say that. After a second, he decided it actually sounded pretty cool, as far as insults go.

"I'm not half as crazy as half this train," Francesca said, "but I must look crazier than I am, or you're thinking I'm at least as crazy as you. We're all crazy, but if you think I'll be drinking that Malört you just forced down straight, then you, Rich, are the craziest of us all. Neat Malört should be outlawed!"

As Rich struggled to process that statement, Francesca continued. "Templeton, I will take three teaspoons of powdered sugar within three measures of Malört, below two measures of ice-cold tap water and a measure of Moxie soda. Stir it for one second, or until the powder looks like milk, then add a stem of some sort. Oh, and I'll take that in a brandy balloon, if you have it. It is the only proper way to drink Malört in society."

Templeton snapped his tiny fingers with a sound like the splash of raindrops, and it wasn't three seconds after the last snap before a tuxedo-wearing centaur galloped into the train car. He rolled a cart ahead of him, upon which sat a silver tray holding two glass brandy balloons, one spoon, a Moxie soda, a stem of some sort, a plate full of sugar cubes, and a carafe of ice-cold tap water. The centaur mixed the drink as Francesca had instructed, then handed it to her. She sipped and nodded in appreciation. The centaur offered Rich a glass of the same bizarre concoction, which he quickly declined. Rich couldn't bear the thought of Malört in any form, watered down or not, sweetened with an entire box of sugar cubes or not. The centaur bowed his head and galloped backward out of the train car.

***

The train traveled swiftly on in some direction.

Francesca sipped her drink calmly, Templeton took deep,

frequent pulls from his bottle, and Rich began to worry. He worried because he couldn't see anything out the windows. It was all just dark underground. He wondered when the next stop was, and where it was.

Francesca sensed his uneasiness. "Don't worry, I ride this train all the time," she said. "It's really only a short ride. The next stop is the last city farm. The stop after that is Dunning Mental Asylum, and after that Riverview Amusement Park. At Riverview, we absolutely must stop in for a Ferris wheel ride or two or three or four. After Riverview, we'll stop in for drinks at the Green Mill Cocktail Lounge before we go to the ball at the Aragon Castle."

"Thanks, it's just I've never been on this train," Rich said. "I've never been through the East Side."

"What sort of music do you like, Rich?" Francesca asked out of the blue.

She wasn't asking him for radio stations, but for some reason, Rich found himself rattling off as many as he could. "Z95, Oldies 104.3, B96, and uh, um, XRT ..." He mumbled something else about Casey Kasem, when Templeton interrupted him, drooling with laughter over Rich's nervous inventory.

Francesca smiled. "You'll be a lord of fraternal lords, Rich, a Greek God of Goldschläger. One day, you'll wake up to the frat marching music of a jam band, and be an Alpha or a Beta, and you'll have forgotten Templeton and me. Isn't that right, Templeton?"

Templeton didn't acknowledge her. He was hunched over, eyes shut, appearing to have laughed himself unconscious.

Francesca went on, "The fraternal sergeant at arms will knead your liver like pizza dough, and this night, our night, will have been formally replaced with a formal, this city you'll have replaced with a dingy frat house, and the lake will be less important to you than a bathtub full of Busch Light. This Lavender Line you'll exchange for the rotting Brown Line, and that'll be the end of you!"

Francesca's face flashed with anger.

That was how she was. One minute, she held Rich's hand, smiling and laughing. The next minute, her tone changed completely, turning dark and foreboding, or just plain crazy. She'd scold Rich for something he hadn't yet done and didn't understand, seemingly at random. Rich didn't know how to react to these outbursts. He didn't read too deeply into them, because he couldn't. He simply came to expect them.

"OK, then. What music do you listen to?" Rich asked her.

"I like Francis O'Neill."

"Francis O'Who? I've never heard of him."

"Francis 'Chief' O'Neill!" Francesca screamed, stirring Templeton. "I'll not dignify such roguery with a response! There's no fairer freehand fluter than the chief!"

Rich thought that if anyone was roguish, it was Francesca and the rest of the Lavender Line. Who were these passengers? The train was a menagerie of every fairy-tale fantasy he'd ever heard of. And where was he? They'd been traveling for at least fifteen minutes and still hadn't emerged from underground, or made any stops. The train had been running a level trek forward, the outside nothing to see but darkness, below or above what, Rich had no idea.

Just as Rich thought this, the train began to slope upward at a faster pace. As it did, the passengers directed their attention to the windows, as if they all expected to surface. A howl from the engine startled Rich. It signaled a final acceleration, before the train burst forth into the night air onto a vast plain, dotted with the lights of little houses, like a countryside landscape at night. Rich saw the city skyline, barely visible over the eastern horizon, the buildings shining like the tips of candle flames. From the location of downtown, Rich could tell the train was traveling south along some far western edge of the city that didn't look like the city at all.

"Let's open the windows," Francesca suggested.

She leaned over Templeton and pulled open a window. The moment she did, a wind burst through the train, transforming the center aisle into a wind tunnel through which Templeton's brown paper bag spiraled into the abyss, along with several hats, a newspaper, hundreds of napkins, and a plate of sugar cubes. Strangely, none of the passengers appeared the least bit bothered by the wind. It was as if it were just another odd guest. Rich didn't mind the wind, either. He liked the sound of it. He had a window next to his bed in his apartment, guarded by a gargantuan, leaf-filled tree. On summer nights, he'd crack the window, and the wind would shuffle the leaves, composing little songs, the leaves' shadows dancing above his bed. He dreamed of the shadows climbing in bed with him, whispering, helping him to sleep.

The wind would help him to sleep again on the train that night. Soon, it had made him drowsy, and the Malört had made him dizzy. His eyelids grew heavy. He struggled to stay awake. He considered falling asleep, but was afraid. He worried Francesca might abandon him, and he'd wake up at the last stop, or somewhere else far, far away.

"Sweat dreams," Templeton slurred.

Then Francesca said something to Rich. It seemed to him that her lips were moving, but no sound came from her mouth. Was the wind muffling her voice? Rich spoke back tiredly, mumbling for her to repeat herself. Francesca drew closer, and said whatever she had said again. Rich still couldn't hear her, so he kept up his mumbling, his eyes barely open. They continued like this, back and forth, Francesca inching ever closer, until she was face to face with him, and he was on the brink of unconsciousness.

Rich would never know for certain what happened next. He liked to think she kissed him, and he kissed her back, but this was doubtful. If there was a kiss, it was only a goodnight kiss. Still, he would have liked to have known whether it happened or not. If so, it was perfectly timed, bestowed the moment he fell asleep and not a second before. At the time he would have received the kiss, he was already flying through the sky, a roguish coat of arms in the wind.

The wind talked to him in his last boyish dream, if he wasn't already dreaming.

Wind of the Windy City, Self-Portrait

The Poisoning of George Gipp
by Thumbelina

You people used to love riddles. Not so much anymore. I don't mind a wily riddle, but then I'm an old-timer, older than the oldest time your old man ever contemplated. No, I don't mind the riddle at all. It's a suitable means of introduction for me, so why don't we play that game, despite you.

Who am I?

> I've felt you and you wonder how,
> You've heard my voice, might hear it now
> I'll whisper and sing a perfect pitch
> I'll bite and scream and howl and bitch
> I've passed through heaven all unseen
> The simple spirit, no king or queen
> Swimming through sky like a fish through sea

I am Wind, and Wind means me!

***

I may fly fancifully, but *this* is a flight of fancy:

> *One FREEZING night, George Gipp stayed out past campus curfew. When he returned to campus, he found himself locked out of his dormitory, on account of the late hour. On these late-night, locked-out occasions, Gipp stayed in the campus theater building. The rear door of the theater building was generally unlocked, but on this particular night, it was strangely locked. Gipp had nowhere to go. He was forced to sleep in the cold outside, and in doing so, contracted pneumonia. The pneumonia would be the official cause of his death some weeks later.*

I have heard truer lies from the inventor of lies. I froze red foxes blue with warmer gusts than the legions I invaded the Midwest with on the night Gipp allegedly stayed outside. Had he truly slept in my company that night, he would have awoken an ice statue.

They call me the slayer of George Gipp, but I played no part. It was a tiny whore who poisoned his blood!

***

I do not recall the exact date, or any date, for that matter. I lose track of time, all the time. An age may pass for me as quickly as a turn of the earth for you. I only know it was winter. It had to have been. I was spry as ever.

The day started as any other. I raced a ghost northeast through the ghost towns of the Great Plains, passing through Missouri before turning sharply north and into the realm of

Gipp. When I finally met him, I was a handsome gust, almost as handsome as Gipp himself. He was impossible to miss there on a grassy field by the lake, playing football. I will not say I targeted him, but he was on my mind.

I came down all blustery, piercing the tiniest chinks in the thickest of garments, sending most of the spectators fleeing for a fire. You would have mistaken a nearby cornfield for a yellow ocean, the way I made waves among the stalks, bending them here and there. Gipp, though, he was a sturdy soul. He would not be bothered with me. He was busy playing the last play of the last game, within the last act of his life. And he won it, with my help. It was I who escorted his final throw into the hands of the receiver. After the game, Gipp gave punting lessons to some raggedy orphans, intentionally missing the team bus back to campus.

I wondered what he had planned.

The moon shone an eerie spotlight upon Gipp that night, stalking him with me, closing about him like the pale twin of his own shadow. Moonlight glowed around him as he made his way into a little farm-town tavern nestled under some train tracks. Gipp remained at the tavern awhile, until the night truly blackened, the way it used to truly blacken.

The tavern looked like an old ship captain's cabin, all musty and wooden and old. *Everything* was old. The people were old. The booze was old. The music was old—an old-timer who looked damned near as old as me was responsible for the music. A whisper from me would have blown that old man clear off the old bench where he sat, behind an old piano, playing old ballads of blackbirds, ballyshannons, and black velvet bands.

Gipp was the young man in the old man's bar. He sat there, drinking stale Blatz beer, jerking his head to attention every time the rusty entry bell chimed above the door. It was easy to see from the way Gipp jerked time and time again, more and more frustrated each time, that he had planned on meeting someone special there, someone who was not there. Several old men offered the young Gipp a drink, and though he did not refuse, he would not entertain any serious conversation. He was angry. He was stood up.

Gipp drank until his heartache was drowned in a sea of Blatz. Then, he leapt out of his old seat and out of the old tavern, toward the whistle of an approaching passenger train. He dashed for the train with life-or-death speed, which now, having said it, sounds rather strange. You see, had he missed that train, his life, I think, would have been much longer. But he did not miss it. He caught it, by a hair. That train would carry him to his contagious angel, the source of his eventual demise.

The train chugged stubbornly southward against my will, ever closer to that windy city named in my honor. I spied Gipp's handsome face within the little round window of his passenger car. He was cozily drinking copious amounts of cognac and applejack. A strange concoction, I thought. He drank and watched the flurries outside defy gravity at my behest. I beat particularly hard against his own little round window. He noticed me then, gazed at me through the glass with glassy eyes, and, like so many others, looked right through me.

I beat the train into the city, first whistling a sad lament through the graves of Graceland, then an even sadder one passing between the old pennants above Wrigley Field. I made my way straight south down Western Avenue, finally to the downtown, where I busied myself defiling a stockbroker's hairpiece outside the Board of Trade. I rediscovered Gipp not far from there, staggering the most drunken stagger down Dearborn Street. He had a hope about him, something the other misfits I blew about like trash on the late-night city streets did not have. It was a hopeless hope of the sort you get drinking and thinking. Drinking and thinking produces strange results. He walked with the hope through the old red-light district, to the front stoop of the notorious Everleigh Club.

The Everleigh Club was the brothel of brothels in its heyday, the capital of New World whorehouses. But that was before Gipp was born. By the time Gipp had come of age, the greatness of the place was gone in everything except the name. Everleigh had become a haven for the sex trade's old and damaged. I could taste the venereal disease on my lips simply blowing against the curtains.

Gipp rapped his huge fists on the Everleigh's front door, with a force that shook the tattered whorehouse's foundation. A few of the butterflies (yes, butterflies) scurried to the windows facing the street and peered down at him. One could see the term "butterfly" was deceiving—most of the women had a mothish look about them.

The butterflies cackled and jeered at Gipp with distorted faces and empty eyes. Gipp beat his chest in a primal way, but looked ridiculous. His motor function had surrendered itself to the will of the cognac, applejack, and Blatz. He wobbled as if he were on the galley of a ship in the roughest of seas.

Soon, a girl no bigger than Thumbelina opened the front door, and I'll call her that, if only to call her something, because I was never certain of her name. I can't overemphasize the tininess of Thumbelina. She would have been prey to the smallest of eagles. She clutched a filthy, cum-stained, rose-patterned bathrobe about her, and stared at Gipp with that look of wide-eyed wonder possible only within the eyes of the young. This Thumbelina was the one Gipp had been waiting for in the old tavern. Gipp tried to but couldn't hide a relieved smile at the sight of her. She helped him up the steps and into the shadows of the Everleigh.

I spent that night watching the vagrants and virgins enter and exit the club. A rule within whorehouses is to serve the men as quickly as possible; the quicker the turnaround, the greater the revenue. Gipp was an exception. I guess he was no ordinary customer. He spent the entire night with Thumbelina. It was not until I felt the deceitful glow of the winter sun across the lake that I saw his face again.

In the morning sun, Gipp's face was the palest color of white I'd ever seen on living skin. There was already a tinge of ghost in him. Thumbelina's sickness was coursing through his veins, quickened by his own thin blood. I sensed the abnormality about Thumbelina from the moment I touched her. An affliction budded fast within her. The disease she had, it was not the usual sort these butterflies contracted in the course of doing business. She had poisoned her flower-fairy prince with it, and he would wither from it.

***

I snuck into Gipp's hospital room not three weeks later, a mere draft. What a state he was reduced to! For a moment, I considered the possibility that I had once again lost track of time. Since I had last seen him, in his prime, the handsome Gipp on that field by the lake, it seemed he had aged a century or more. He reeked of the pestilence Thumbelina had bestowed that night.

There exists an account of an inspirational parting speech Gipp delivered in his final moments, to a friend named Rock. Your history tells it like this:

> *I've got to go, Rock. It's all right. I'm not afraid. Sometime, Rock, when the team is up against it, when things are wrong and the breaks are beating the boys, ask them to go in there with all they've got and win just one for the Gipper. I don't know where I'll be then, Rock. But I'll know about it, and I'll be happy.*

Your history is a lie.

I heard the true last words spoken by Gipp. They were the words of a nonsense verse. The true words may have been less mythical than those of the liar's tale, but they were far lovelier. This is what he actually said:

Chase me, halfback. I've got cognac. Up the leg of me drawers.
If you don't believe me. Come and feel me. Up the leg of me
drawers.

I prefer the nonsense verse. After he spoke it, Gipp stared for a while out the window at me. I came to him, caressing his face gently with a zephyr. It gave him a settled finish.

I went shrieking outside through the sky that night, as Gipp fell asleep comfortably sheltered from me in his deathbed. I'm certain that when he closed his eyes for the last time, he was dreaming one last dream of his tiny butterfly from the Everleigh. I wondered if he pictured her blowing about in my arms, a tiny tumbleweed through the Midwest. I wondered if she dreamt of him. I wondered if butterflies dreamt at all.

***

I visited Gipp's cemetery once, before the onset of a thunderstorm, late one otherwise lazy summer afternoon. The dark clouds hovered like giant, fluffy capacitors as I spun cartwheels and danced whirlwinds on the Gipp grave. I swirled about until all the cemetery was empty of living guests. Performing for the dead was never my forte, so I burst forth across Lake Michigan, wrecking an ill-timed game of spades between four decaying seamen on the bow of a festering freighter. I remember the confused looks on their grizzled faces when I claimed their deck of cards, as if in a magic trick. It served the halfwits right, playing cards on the deck of a ship, with me all around!

The thunder grumbled at them, as if to say, "Don't you know the wind, the wind in the windy city?"

And the thunder grumbled again.

Oberon, Titania and Puck with Fairies Dancing

Night Dance of the Wild Kings

Rich awoke to the grumble of thunder left over from summer. He didn't realize it was a leftover, until Francesca told him it was. She said it had to be a leftover because of how loud it *wasn't*. She said you could always recognize a leftover thunder for how loud it wasn't.

The wind had been shut out from the train, left alone in the rain. All the windows were closed on account of the suddenly stormy weather. Rich looked out at the dead cornfields under the lightning light and wanted to be in the wide-open air, wet as it was. He'd been shut inside the city for too long.

As Rich looked out the window, he noticed a white figure drifting through the sky. He couldn't tell what it was at first. It was too big to be a bird, but much too small to be a plane. It floated about in the most unpredictable way, skipping from star to star, in and out of storm clouds, sliding down lightning bolts, then falling with the rain, closer and closer to the train, until it was so close, Rich was surprised to see it was a little girl wearing a white dress.

"Isn't the night rain pretty, Rich?" Francesca asked.

Rich turned toward Francesca, who was still sipping her drink. He saw Templeton had fallen back asleep, or passed out. His tiny elf body was sprawled out on the seat next to Francesca, and a dribble of what looked like vomit hung from his chin. Rich turned back to the window, trying to regain sight of the flying girl, but he couldn't find her anywhere. He guessed she'd flown away.

"Isn't the night rain pretty, Rich?" Francesca asked again.

Rich was surprised to see the storm here and there and everywhere. Before he'd fallen asleep, it was nowhere, not a cloud in sight. "When did it start raining?" he asked.

"You woke up the minute the storm started, just after we closed the windows. What do you prefer, Rich, a night rain or a night train?"

"What?"

"You may like both. Just now, we're in a night train in a night rain, or riding a train in the rain through the night. Would you agree with that?"

"I think I, I … I think I had a dream, but I can't remember anything about it."

"Tell me what you remember. What kind of dream was it? Was it an ordinary daydream? A redream? A midsummer night's dream? It wasn't an American dream, was it? I hate the American ones. City dreams are really so much more interesting, sad as they all end."

Rich's dream was one of those elusive ones, instantly forgotten the moment you awake from it. He couldn't remember a single detail, except that it was worth remembering. Rich wondered where the memories of dreams hid, and why his lips tasted so sweet.

"Rich, I've just now asked you at least seven questions in a row, and you've not answered one. What has gotten into you?"

Francesca next said something she was sure would capture Rich's attention. "I dreamed a dream myself, as you were dreaming. Mine was just a bit of a daydream. Would you like to hear it? It was about you, after all, so you should hear it."

Of course, Rich had never been more interested in anything in his life. It was the first time a beautiful girl (or any girl) like Francesca had dreamt of him. Unfortunately for Rich, the dream wouldn't turn out to be the sort he'd hoped for. Francesca wasn't even in the dream. Still, he'd take it over nothing.

Here was how she explained it:

> *You were at a bar downtown called Stocks and Blondes. You were old and fat and disgusting and had just gotten off work from your miserable job as a vice president of something, which is how you'll end up, sorry to say, but such is the life path of a jam-band-listening fraternal businessman of business. Seen it a thousand times. Anyway, you argued with your wife on the phone about something. You were promising her you wouldn't stay out late fucking your co-workers or something, but you definitely intended to fuck one or more of your co-workers. At least one. Your wife said you would be pissed as lord off your*

fizzy cross of gold, and she was right. You would be pissed, though you promised her you would not. The wind blew you home with the storm at some ungodly hour of the night. You were so drenched in sex you would have guessed it was the flavor of the rain bucketing down. You had a son at home, and you acted like one yourself. Your son liked that in you. Your wife, not so much. Your wife went practically mad waiting for you that night. You'd crossed the line one time too many, she said to herself, but she said that all the time. Later that night, you snuck out of bed, and your wife thought, sneaky devil, always sneaking around. You'd become a master at leaving places unnoticed. Your returns, on the other hand, were a chorus of ninety-nine bottles of beer on the wall, all drunk and disorderly. Your wife searched the house for you. She found you where she expected to find you, in your little man's room. You called your son "little man," but he was no little man, he was a wild thing. Just as wild as you. The two of you were like wild kings in that house. Your wife can't imagine the boy ending up like his dad, but he will. Squinting through the keyhole of the boy's room, she couldn't see anything until a flash of leftover lightning exposed you. You were standing near the window with the boy's Spider-Man pajamas knotted around you like tangled red vine. The boy had your fancy businessman necktie wrapped around his head like a crown. You giggled together, "I had this dream. We

*danced a dance, even the fairy, who crawled up my
pants." The two of you danced around the room, and
your wife wished to be you, or at least to join you.
She walked in and asked if she might dance with you,
and the three of you danced one last dance.*

Rich could only wonder at what dreams meant.

***

The Lavender Line took an abrupt turn east, toward the city.
The cat conductor strolled through the train roaring his
announcement, "NEXT STOP, LAST CHICAGO FARM,
LAST CHICAGO FARM UP NEXT!"

Rich figured they must be well outside the city if they
were stopping at a farm. He looked out the window, where
he saw the dark storm clouds give way to the remnants of
afterglow. Above the faded colors, in a gray patch of sky, he
saw the white figure of the little girl again, sailing here and
there as she had before. Rich couldn't take his eyes off her.
It was the first time he'd seen anyone drifting through the
sky.

The train made its first stop. The depot was no more
than a little red stone cottage with a thatched roof. Only one
passenger entered their car. He was a middle-aged man
dressed in clothes that looked pulled straight from the closet
of Jay Gatsby: a plain white collared dress shirt, red
suspenders, brown Oxford bag pants, and a felt top hat. He
clinched a long, silver, full-bent, ladle-looking pipe in his
teeth, which were hardly visible through his blond walrus

mustache. He was all wet from the storm. He sat next to Rich, checked the time on his pocket watch, and relit his pipe. Francesca greeted him.

"Good evening, sir. I am Francesca Finnegan, and this is Rich Lyons. What is your name and where are you traveling this evening?"

"A fine evening to you both," the man said. "My name is Doctor Harvey Denlinger. My destination is my place of business, Dunning Mental Asylum. Where are you—" The doctor paused mid-sentence, for he had noticed Templeton sprawled out on the seat, unconscious.

"It appears this elf is in need of medical attention."

At that, Templeton temporarily regained consciousness and spat on the floor in the doctor's direction.

"Well, I never!" the doctor gasped.

"It's all right," Francesca explained. "He is a hero, after all."

"A hero! His hero days look well behind him. As I was saying, where are you off to this evening?" The doctor stared suspiciously at Templeton.

"We are on our way to a ball at the Aragon Castle," Francesca said excitedly. "Before we go there, I think we may stop off at Riverview for a ride on the Ferris wheel, and after, maybe a cocktail at the Green Mill Cocktail Lounge."

"If this weather clears, there is no better night for Riverview," the doctor said. "A spin through the city stars on the Ferris wheel! Oh, how I miss it, and maybe a shake of the Ferris wheel car for good measure, eh? No better cause for closeness!" The doctor looked at Rich with his eyebrows raised. "And a cocktail to follow at the Green Mill, maybe a note of music to go with it? What a night that would make, what a fine night indeed!"

Rich wasn't paying any attention to the doctor. He'd hardly even noticed the man sit down next to them, because he'd once again found the girl in the sky. When the train started to move, continuing east, it seemed as if the flying girl flew along with the train, dancing a private dance through the sky, just for Rich. At one point, she came so close, Rich thought he'd locked eyes with her.

Rich motioned for the doctor and Francesca to peer out the window at the spectacle in the sky, which they did. The doctor wasn't the least bit surprised.

"Hmmm. Yes, of course, a patient of mine is a relation, the brother actually, of that flying damsel. She was recently caught in a tornado and has yet to return to the ground. It's the damnedest thing. Her brother is mental over it, and I mean that in a literal sense. He has completely lost his wits. I'd like nothing more than for her to land. She is quite the gifted artist, you know."

As Rich watched the girl fly above the dark fields, he began to doubt his own sense of time. Not the time of night. He didn't care about that. He had no curfew, and his mother was already asleep. He doubted his own sense of where *in* time he was. The doctor, the flying girl, the Lavender Line, and everything that had happened since he'd met Francesca didn't quite fit in the present. Everything belonged to the city, but to some other time of the city. The landscape outside the train windows didn't look like the city at all. If that was the city outside, it was the city when it was young.

"What's the flying girl's name?" Rich asked the doctor.

"Why, she is Billy Boyle, queen of the last Chicago farm."

*She wore a pretty white dress, whiter than baking soda
or this shiny white floor*

Queen of the Last Chicago Farm

The story of Billy Boyle takes place long ago, when Chicago was less windy and had rather narrow shoulders. Back then, it wasn't anywhere near a second city. It wasn't even a top ten. In fact, it was barely a city at all. It had forests, fields, and farms. Well, just one farm, but it was an important farm. It was the last city farm. Billy was queen on that farm.

Queen Billy was not a famous painter, though she did paint a famous picture.

***

The clinical psychologist Doctor Harvey Denlinger of Dunning Mental Asylum began his day peering down at the patient intake detail from the previous night's admissions over a cup of coffee. He looked over the intake, wondering whom he should evaluate first. He had some interesting options.

> **Adam Aleweidat**, *32. Cut each of his feet off with a tree-pruning saw in a fit of religious hysteria. "I think I need no feet to walk in heaven. If I do, they will grow back."*

Martin Stachura, *28. Claimed to be Robin (Hood) of Loxley when found passed out drunk on the doorstep last night. Now claims only to have been hypnotized by Robin Hood. CPD have armed robbery warrant for him.*

Anand Reddy, *33. Emaciated opium addict, found overnight, sleeping in Aladdin's Castle within Riverview Amusement Park. Claims to see lions and tigers in the wind. Room windows must be kept shut at all times. Believes he can fly.*

Megan McGuane, *19. Silly, wild Irish stray, reappearing here periodically under the strangest of circumstances. CPD found her "wandering through a Wicker Park alley fully nude, in search of a prince to whom she is supposedly betrothed." Discovered her fornicating with new patient, Martin Stachura (Prince of Thieves), in holding room shortly after admission.*

Arlo Boyle, *18. Transferred from Northwestern Hospital, where he was treated for injuries received during North Side tornado. Tornado killed his entire family and destroyed their farm. Stares out the window constantly.*

It was an easy choice for the doctor. He grew up on a farm himself. He would see Arlo Boyle first.

***

Doctor Denlinger stood outside Boyle's room, spying on him through a peephole in the steel door. Boyle had the slim frame of a boy, with the weather-beaten complexion of a man, under bushy red hair that matched the color of his overalls. He looked as sane as anyone, sitting there with an unlit cigarette in his hand, squinting out the window, looking about curiously, as if he were simply bird watching. He reminded Doctor Denlinger of Huckleberry Finn.

The doctor entered cautiously. "Pleased to meet you, Mr. Boyle. I'm your doctor, Doctor Harvey Denlinger, but please call me Harvey. My condolences on the loss of your family and farm."

Boyle looked startled by the sudden entrance. He turned away from the window and faced the ground, nervously fingering his cigarette.

"Allow me to light your cigarette, sir." Doctor Denlinger pulled a matchbook from his coat pocket. The doctor-patient bond was formed in the instant the match caught fire. The doctor pulled up a chair. Boyle sat on the end of his bed, still looking toward the window, taking long drags of the cigarette.

"Thank you, doctor. The cigarette smoke makes me feel spry as wild rye under a stormy sky, as my father would say. Hey, why don't they let you have no matches in here, anyway? I can have these here cigarettes, but no matches. Crazy rules for us crazies, meant to make us more crazy? Is that so, Doctor Harvey?" Boyle turned to look at Doctor Denlinger.

"It is a policy of my own recommendation, put in place

to protect certain patients from themselves," the doctor replied. "I'll make an exception in your case and see to it you have some matches from here on out. How does that sound?"

Boyle gave a slight nod in appreciation, and the doctor began his line of questioning.

"All right, then, let's get started. I see your address is here in Chicago. I confess I was surprised when I saw you were in the city proper. I didn't realize any farmers still resided within the city limits. What kind of farm is it?"

Boyle gave the doctor a sidelong squint. "You mean to say what kind of farm *was* it?"

"Yes, yes of course, my apologies." Doctor Denlinger silently cursed himself for the mistake. "What happened the day of the tornado? Would you feel comfortable discussing that with me?"

Boyle shrugged his shoulders in an apathetic sort of way. The doctor set his coffee down and prepared his pen and notepad dutifully. Boyle somehow smoked and talked at the same time.

"My baby sister, Billy, proclaimed herself queen of the farm, and I chief in her service. I put a crown of golden leaves upon her head and she was more delighted than if the thing was studded with real diamonds. Her and I sat playing in a mound of those golden leaves under this lonely tall tree in the middle of a wide cornfield. There is no lovelier sound than the swish-swoosh of cornstalks in a field of wind. It is like music to the ears of a farmer. I imagine the sound to be like the breaking of waves to an islander. There was that wonderful wind blowing the stalks musically, as we took turns throwing the leaves as high as we might into the sky. Billy danced in happy circles as they fell on her, but her fun would not last. The last bundle of leaves went into the sky, never to come back to the ground. I remember wondering at how strange that was."

Boyle took a long puff of the cigarette as he roamed back to the window, looking up, down, left, right, before continuing.

"As I looked for the lost leaves in the sky, I noticed the onset of a moving shadow out some way west, changeful in its course, darting this way and that at random. I couldn't see no tornado in the shadow, so thought not much of it. It just looked unnatural. Not that I'd have known a tornado if I saw one. We ain't seen a tornado in the history of the farm, so was not prepared whatsoever. Sure a farm in Oklahoma got a storm shelter and all that, but what we got, Doctor Harvey? We ain't got shit. Not even a basement."

"I understand," the doctor said. "I grew up on an Iowa farm. We had no storm shelter, either. Tornadoes this far north are uncommon. Do go on."

"Billy dressed for the coronation that day. She wore a pretty white dress, whiter than baking soda or this shiny white floor. I will not forget how it flapped all over in the wind as we ran through the cornfield in a panic, cornered without corners. The rows of cornstalks were endless. There was no end and no shelter. As the winds strengthened, we hunkered down together under that lonely tree with little hope. The storm passed just near us, and started pulling us toward it, pulling her from me. As Billy began sliding away, I got on my feet and grabbed hold of her wrists as tightly as I could manage. The force of the wind pulled her so hard, her body was splayed out flat in the air, as if she lay on an invisible bed, and I stood at the end of it pulling her. I stood and played tug of war with the storm for what seemed many minutes, and in the winds of the tornado, I saw the shape of a grinning face like a wind spirit swirling to and fro, just like he was fuckin' with me."

Boyle paused, allowing the doctor time to catch up on his notes. The doctor noted the story, and also how Boyle's voice shifted from poetic to countryish and colloquial. The doctor thought these might be early symptoms of a dissociative disorder.

Boyle took a powerful finishing drag of his cigarette before starting again.

"I'd have kept hold of her, had the chicken coop not exploded into a trillion feathers, but that's just what happened when the cyclone landed on it. The sky was a goddamned blizzard of chicken feathers. I saw many a flying chicken and chick. It was a magical sight, those flying chickens, stranger than any dream you ever dreamt. The feathers blinded me, filled my mouth, and clogged my nose. It was then I lost her. As the chicken feathers cleared from my eyes, I saw her, drifting away. She did not spiral about in a wild sort of way. She floated away from the earth, ascending high in the storm, and in her white dress against the black clouds, she might have been mistook for an angel, were it not for the surprised look on her face."

Boyle walked to the window and looked out again.

"I am sorry to hear your story, Mr. Boyle. It was a terrible storm, destroyed everything from Wilmette southeast down Foster Avenue to the lake. One of our own nurses was off the shore boating on the lake when it struck. She has still not been found."

"Do you hold out hope for that nurse? Nothing has been found of Billy, not even her crown of leaves, or that white dress. I think she may turn up yet."

The doctor paused in thought at Boyle's comment, then questioned him further.

"Is that why you look out the window? Are you looking for your sister in the sky?"

"Sure it is, and why not? She can't have landed on the fuckin' moon. I think she is likely hard to see in her white dress against these white clouds. Look up there." Boyle pointed toward the clouds. "Clouds white, same as her dress."

Doctor Denlinger scribbled some concluding notes, looked at his watch, and rose to leave. He had a schedule to keep, and had to be on to his next patient.

Boyle clung to the conversation. "What you do when you ain't doctoring, Doctor Harvey?"

"Very little. I spend most of my time here at Dunning. The free time I do have is spent in various advisory capacities throughout the city. Most recently I have been appointed to lead the municipal flag commission. We are tasked with determining the future flag of this fine city."

Boyle's eyes widened, and he became suddenly excited.

"Billy is a drawer! She draws all sorts of drawings. Even painted some! Her drawings are here between the pages of this journal. It's something I found in the rubble. Will you look at them with me? You may find your flag in here."

Doctor Denlinger humored Boyle, sitting beside him for several minutes as they quickly flipped through hundreds of pages of mostly farm landscapes, sketched with a pencil. The doctor found himself surprised at the quality of certain pictures. One in particular caught his eye. It was a painting of four red stars set against a background of two blue stripes and three white stripes.

"I do admire this painting," Doctor Denlinger said. "What is it meant to represent? What are these red stars?"

"Those there are stars, doctor, red dwarfs to be sure. I'm not a lettered man, but I know my stars, as I thought did any farmer. With the stars above, we don't need a proper calendar to determine the day. A fully bright Orion signals winter, as does the Summer Triangle with spring. A calendar tells me nothing a harvest moon can't."

"It would appear my knowledge of astronomy, for a farmer's son, is embarrassingly poor. Why does she paint the red dwarf in particular?"

"The stars stand for me, mom, dad, and Billy. There is one star to stand for each of us. Dad always said that as Chicago farmers, we had much in common with the red dwarf. See it's a rare thing to see a red dwarf. They're at the end of their life span, much like the city farmer."

"It is a clever comparison and a proper, beautiful family sigil. It's true, the typical Chicagoan has never seen a red dwarf in the sky, nor met a farmer. I've met my farmer today. Perhaps I'll look up to the sky for a red dwarf tonight!"

Boyle didn't acknowledge the comment. He was staring out the window intently.

The doctor looked again at the picture. "And what do these blue stripes mean?"

"She was queen, as I said. Queen Billy. That is her blue blood."

"Might I borrow this, just this one drawing, Mr. Boyle?"

Boyle gave him the picture, but only after the doctor promised to return it. Should Queen Billy land safely, she would want it back.

***

Doctor Denlinger fell so in love with the girl's painting, he unveiled the design at his next municipal council meeting, where he proposed it for consideration as the future flag of the city. He changed only the symbolism of the picture, associating it with the city, rather than the farm. The red stars would each represent milestones in city history: Fort Dearborn, the Great Chicago Fire, the World's Columbian Exhibition, and, later, the Century of Progress exhibition. The blue stripes would represent Lake Michigan and the Chicago River, and the white stripes would represent the North, West, and South Sides of Chicago[4]. The council voted unanimously to adopt the design, and it has gone on to become the city flag many recognize today.

---

[4] *The East Side is still not represented within the Chicago flag today.* ☺

And so, the last Chicago farm delivered in its destruction the symbol that would represent the new and thriving city, soon to become the place we now know—the great capital of the Midwest, with no memory or evidence of any farms or their queens. The flag's unfurling marked the total urbanization of the city, fittingly born from and stained with the blue blood of the queen of the last Chicago farm.

Anyone after claiming to be a farmer in Chicago would have to be committed, just as Arlo Boyle was, because there are no farms left in the city, not unless you count the roots.

What do you intend to do? Will you ask me to ride the Ferris wheel,
or will you ask the Ferris wheel to ride me?

Apparition of an Amusement Park

The flying queen disappeared with the storm as the Lavender Line continued eastward through the strange city countryside.

"What's the time, Francesca?" Rich asked.

"Time as in the date, the time of night, or that one time?"

"Um, everything, I guess, except for that one time."

"Let's see, the time, the time. Time? Now that I think of it, I'm not exactly sure of the time. I can't remember the last time I even thought of time, to be honest. In the East Side, there are years when nothing happens, and minutes when years happen. On the Lavender Line, there are rides where minutes pass forward in one direction, and other rides where decades pass backward in the other direction. It's all just like white noise, see what I mean?"

Rich was quiet for a while as he tried to work out what she'd said. Of course he couldn't, so he tried to ask the question differently.

"What time would a clock say, right now?"

"I met a clock once at a party, and he had very little to say. When I asked the clock the time, he sarcastically told me he'd of course need a mirror to tell, what with the time being on his face and all. The clock declared himself wasted, saying there was nothing so common in this world as wasted time. Time is wasted all the time. We waste time then time wastes us. The clock also said quite seriously that the past and future were just thoughts of things that had already happened, or were about to happen, so why care anything about the matter at all? I tend to agree with the clock. Clocks know time, after all."

***

Francesca wrote with her unpolished fingertips on the fogged train window:

knird nekat sah eh, fle siht dniM

"Little reminder for the conductor when we're gone. He reads from the outside in, like most feline train conductors. Just don't call him dyslexic. You'll get a claw to the face for saying something like that."

The conductor roared his cat roar, "DUNNING NEXT STOP, DUNNING MENTAL ASYLUM!" The only passenger who prepared himself for exit at Dunning was the doctor.

"I say, my stop already. I must be on the way."

Francesca proposed a toast, but the doctor would have none of it.

"I am working the night shift tonight. Must be spry as wild rye under a stormy sky, as a farmer would say. No drink for me, but don't let it stop you. If I get off early, I shall report to the Aragon for a libation."

"Cheers to you, Doctor Denlinger of the Dunning delirious." Francesca raised her glass. Templeton twitched. Rich just sort of nodded his head.

"Here, here. Before my departure, if I may request one thing further from each of you. Keep your eyes up to the sky. Should you encounter the flying girl in your travels this evening or after, I'd only ask for you to inform her of the fact that we have her brother in custody at Dunning, and that he is most distressed at her arbitrarily drifting about the atmosphere."

Francesca and Rich agreed they would.

The doctor bowed a farewell as the train stopped. Rich wiped a viewing circle in the condensed window to get a look at Dunning. He didn't remember it snowing out, so was surprised to see a sparkling white blanket of snow covering the wide fenced-in grounds of the institution. Dunning itself was an extremely long, cathedral-shaped building, which looked to Rich like a haunted house. There wasn't a single soul in sight, within or without. A sign outside a narrow front gate read:

Cook County Insane Asylum, Est. 1869

"Looks like an old church went for a walk and got lost, or possessed," Rich said. "Didn't know there was a mental institution right here in the city."

Francesca's voice lowered. "It's a tomb for the living. A graveyard for the unwanted. Thousands buried everywhere around here. Probably even under these train tracks. No one knows it or gives a damn, not that they would if they knew."

"If no one knows it, how do you know?"

"I just know what I know. And you know what you know, which is less than what I know. All you know are the lies you're taught by liars who've been taught by other liars who've been taught lies by liars. It's a vicious cycle of lying and dying. I know the truth. Did you know most anything that matters in this city was built by magic before it was built by men? Of course you didn't. This city is different from other cities. The true history of it is unpublished. Lucky for you, I know it all by heart."

***

The train left Dunning, progressing steadily along a high pass on a narrow ridge, surrounded by tall trees on either side. The countryside faded away. Rich was relieved at the familiar sight of city alleyways beyond the trees, and the bungalows beyond them. This was a neighborhood he knew, or thought he knew, but there was something different about it. Everything was much less crowded. There were too many trees within too many parks, beside too few apartments. And was the sky above darker, or were there fewer city lights?

"Have you ever been to Riverview?" Francesca asked Rich.

"River who?"

"Riverview Amusement Park! The Bobs Roller Coaster, Aladdin's Castle, the Silver Flash! It sits on the river just near the next stop. There's roller coasters, bumper cars, and the oddest oddities: the legless lady, the educated elephant, the werewolf woman, and a hundred others. Oh, and the greatest Ferris wheel you've ever seen! Have you ever ridden a Ferris wheel? Will you ride the Ferris wheel with me? We can see the lake from the highest height if the weather's all right."

"How can you be so sure Riverview is still open? Summer's been over two months now. And it looks like it just snowed."

"You're despicably unadventurous tonight, not counting the sip of Malört you took and the jumping into the river after me, but who wouldn't do that. It's not too late, we're just running late. Next stop Riverview!"

The train made a sudden, steep descent into woods so thick, the tree branches on either side clung to the windows, darkening the interior of the train and forcing it to slow considerably. Rich could see it had been a long time since the train had traveled those tracks. They plowed through the overgrowth, jolting and bumping and banging like crazy. The bumping and banging made Rich nervous. For one terrifying second, he thought he actually saw a pair of giant branch-like hands among the trees, groping at the window, along with two glowing green eyes. Rich was relieved when the woods finally became less suffocating.

"RIVERVIEW THIS STOP, LAUGH YOUR TROUBLES AWAY, RIVERVIEW!"

The train stopped in a glade near the entrance to the amusement park. Rich and Francesca left Templeton in his passed-out state, and stepped out of the train into the night. It was noticeably colder out, but there was no snow. The park entrance gate towered over them, its two pillars like miniature Kremlins, each with an onion dome on top. The park through the gates looked enormous. Rich wondered how it was he'd never been there.

Before they started toward the park, Rich glanced back at the train. Francesca's writing was now legible on the window where they'd sat:

Mind this elf, he has taken drink

The park looked empty, yet fully alight and operational. Francesca led Rich through the entrance, where Rich expected a park employee to ask him for his ticket, but there was no employee to be found, anywhere. There wasn't anyone anywhere. The lights were lit and the rides rode, all without any people.

They strolled through the park holding hands, stopping here or there for this or that. They played Skee-Ball and Pop-a-Shot. They ate elephant ears and cotton candy served by no one, yet there for anyone. They rode the teacup and the octopus alone together. It seemed as though the park was open for them, but closed to everyone else.

They made their way to a far edge of the park, where they saw a Ferris wheel spinning strangely all alone, separated from the rest of the attractions. A dark river, flecked with red and yellow spots from the falling leaves, flowed beneath the wheel, beyond which lay a dense forest.

Rich stared at the Ferris wheel. Francesca stared at Rich. "What do you intend to do? Will you ask me to ride the

Ferris wheel, or will you ask the Ferris wheel to ride me?"

"Yes," was all Rich could think to say.

The Ferris wheel stopped on cue as they approached, as if it had seen them coming. The moment they sat together, it jerked forward into motion. It spun as slowly as you'd expect any Ferris wheel to spin. Slow as it was, the ride thrilled Francesca. Each time they reached the highest height, she clutched Rich's skinny arm as if with the fear of death. Rich liked that.

It was pleasant up there, Ferris-wheeling through the night air. The sky cleared of the earlier storm, and a barely visible layer of velvet lay on the far western horizon, reminding Rich it wasn't all that long ago the sun had set. They saw the moon rise above the lake, below unusually bright white stars. Strangely, there were no airplanes in sight. The stars were worth gazing at that night. It seemed to Rich he'd hardly noticed them before, and for that, he felt as if his whole short life had been a shame. He hoped he'd remember to look up at the stars more often, after the ride had ended.

Francesca and Rich circled and circled, then circled again. They might have stayed on the ride until dawn, were it not for the old man. They didn't see him approach, if he approached at all. He appeared suddenly, as if out of thin air, standing underneath the Ferris wheel, staring up at them, unmoving. The ride completed its final rotation and stopped, by no coincidence, at the lowest point of exit, where Rich and Francesca exited.

"Who are you?" the old man croaked. He looked even older up close.

"We are park-goers riding the Ferris wheel," Francesca answered. "Who are you?"

"For the moment, I am Paul A. LaRock the third or fourth, I don't remember which, city-renowned founder of this Riverview Amusement Park. But, only for the moment. As you can see, I soon expect to be the ghost of the Gravitron, if there is not already one."

"Sir, your Ferris wheel is a wonder," Francesca said.

"Thank you, ma'am. It is, you know—a wonder. It truly is. I have come here to ride that Ferris wheel. At my age, you never know which ride will be the last! Did you know, that river below the Ferris wheel, the Chicago River, is the only river in the world to flow backward? It is a little-known fact and rightly so, as no one can believably explain the cause. Engineers would say a complex, man-made system of canals causes this. They are wrong. The flow of the river was established by a single soul. I knew him once, though we haven't met in the longest time, not since the first Roosevelt was president, I think. He is a figure who exists now only in a dream. Can I tell you my dream?"

"I love dreams," Francesca said excitedly.

The old man took a labored breath before beginning.

"I lay half asleep on the third floor of our lakefront estate, facing the open window, through which a curiously strong wind flaps the drapes wildly about the room. I am drawn to the window, not to close it, but to look outside of it. From the window, I peer down onto the whitecaps of Lake Michigan. I see him down there, combing the shoreline, searching frantically about the sand dunes. He finds me up in the window, facing me with his strange stare. I feel a spasm of terror, then wake."

Francesca and Rich remained silent. The old man had more to tell.

"I have heard it said the people of your life who visit you in your dreams have unfinished business with you. I believe that to be true. I think that is maybe why I find myself standing here tonight."

"Why is it you stand here tonight, if not for the Ferris wheel?" Francesca asked.

"For the machinist in those woods beyond the river." The old man pointed toward the forest.

"Tell us about the machinist."

"Ride the Ferris wheel with me, and I will tell you. His story begins and ends with the Ferris wheel anyway."

Monster Selfie

The Riverview Machinist

My amusement park was to be Lord of Lakeview, an attraction beyond the capacity of any imagination. Construction had begun en masse. The assembly of a horse carousel to rival Tivoli's had just started off the corner of Belmont and Western Avenues. I had finalized the design for the park entrance gates. A team of reputable engineers had been selected to build a grand Ferris wheel. It was an exciting time for all involved. My Riverview could not be ready soon enough.

The first of many challenges posed to me in the building of the park was a shortage of timber for general construction. To control costs, I decided to supply extra wood from the adjoining grounds nearest the river. It was a densely wooded area, the trees there survivors of a once vast, now forgotten, forest, with roots so deep I guessed they lined the walls of Satan's bedchamber in the nethermost pits of hell. I retained a clan of vigorous-looking Italians for the specific purpose of clearing those old woods. They were an economical hire, having agreed to workhouse wages along with a lunch ration of red wine and buttered bread.

The initial progress made by the Italians was satisfactory, but short-lived. They became altogether inefficient not three weeks into the project, slowing considerably in their efforts to clear the old woods closest to the river. I figured them nose baggers every last one, likely assuming my coffers bottomless. Well, I'd not have them "nanty narking" on my dime. I scheduled a private conference with an English-speaking representative of the group, a young snoutfair called Camarata.

I harshly rebuked him, his miscreant fellows, and the Latin race in general. When I demanded an excuse for the slow progress, the boy swore upon his nonna that a pair of the Italians had been accosted by an earthen specter! He claimed a small group of workers had been chopping away dutifully when they heard an eerie splash from within the river. From a distance, they observed what they initially believed to be a rider fording the river on a brown steed. Upon closer examination, they believed it to be a supernatural being—giant in size, with mossy skin, buck horns, hair of leaves, and an old man's face. It calmly strode toward them, hoisted a trunk of birch the size of a motor car (allegedly), and flung it at them as though it were no heavier than a twig! The Italians ran from the thing in terror.

As anyone would, I guessed this story to be most fabulously contrived by the Italian con-artist lumberers. Surely they found the whole fiasco entertaining, sending Camarata to me with such an outlandish tale. I dismissed the boy angrily, but not before assuring him that should sufficient progress not be made in the felling of those trees,

I'd be fattening Negro replacements on the Italians' daily rations while they begged for pasta in the streets.

I began personally overseeing the Italians the following dawn. I was pleased to note the effect. It seemed this had been a simple case of "cat away mice will play." In short order, they began making satisfactory progress on the woods.

As was the case during the park's construction, it was the death of one problem, the birth of another. Next were the Ferris wheel engineers. I became seriously concerned with their ability to meet the originally contracted deadline. They had not delivered any preliminary designs for my approval, and I had not been in frequent communication with the principal, a keg-shaped Carpathian called Hans Hasler. I dreamed of Hans linking sausages instead of metal beams, laughing heartily at my expense.

Looking back, it mattered not, as you will see.

***

One perfectly fine day, the Italians did not show up for work. I remember flipping through my calendar, guessing it must have been some Roman Catholic holiday, which I had not considered. To my disgust, it was not, so I set myself to solve the mystery at once. That morning, I searched far and wide throughout the Italian blocks of the Hull House neighborhood to ascertain some likely implausible explanation. I confronted a member of the crew at a shelter (naturally) on Taylor Street.

I expected the mystery to solve itself in the form of a short, pitiful excuse, but it would not be so simple. His

English was difficult to interpret, but I gathered the Italians had been accosted by the same imaginary creature that had been described to me some time ago by the Camarata boy. I offered to increase their hourly wages, but the man would hear none of it. He swore on his pope he would not return to the grounds of the park, even if his family should lie starving in a gutter.

The worker's rant was beyond the superstitious nature of a Latin heart. I concluded there must be some bear living in those woods, or some other outlaws intruding on my land. I therefore readied myself for an adventure into the Devil's forest at dusk the next day, in search of what, I knew not.

***

I had nothing with me but my white shepherd, Welsh Widower (how I miss her), a loaded Sharps buffalo rifle (never too careful), and an oil lantern (eyes in the dark). It was too hot a midsummer's night. The humidity in the air, coupled with the powerful gusts, had me worried my hunt might be postponed by the onset of a storm. The heat forced the blades of grass to bend like skinny green knights in my honor as I marched forth. I could hear the woods wailing a warning as I approached from across the field.

Truth be told, I had never been very deep into those woods, so had some trouble finding a break in the tree line. After much pacing back and forth, I discovered a narrow deer path and strayed down it, toward the river. A short way along the path, a blast of wind breached the thin glass case of my lantern, blowing out the candle, leaving me quite in the dark. I was lucky Welsh Widower had the night vision of a flock of owls, or I'd have died walking into a tree, or the river itself—it did not take us long to reach it.

At the riverbank, I beheld the strangest sight. The river was alight, the air above it a queer galaxy, thick with fireflies reveling, orbiting about like yellow stars. Gazing into the waters, I could see quite clearly what I at first took to be fish, but upon closer observation saw were only the size of fish. These things were like little naked angels dancing about, illuminated from the concentrated nightlights above. It was such a sight, I fell into a swoon there on the edge of the river, and so the time lapse between my arrival at the riverbank and his arrival is difficult for me to surmise. If I could recount minutes as they pass in a dream, I might be able to ascertain how long I stood there, but I cannot. I think it was quite long, before *he* interrupted me.

He approached from the opposite bank of the river, strolling on the goddamned water like Jesus Christ on the Sea of Galilee. The fireflies cleared a path for him, as if by his command. I did not immediately recognize his whole figure. Only his shiny emerald eyes stood out. As he came closer, I saw him and was petrified. He was a beast of a thing, about eight feet tall, with the wide chest of a sportsman. He had a weather-beaten, tree-lichen-covered face beneath a thick red beard, and long hair made of leaves. Out of his head sprouted two fawn horns. He was as the Italians had described him— horrifying. I thought him a woodsy deformity, or the Devil himself come to slay me.

When he drew near enough, I hoisted the buffalo shooter

and commanded he halt, albeit in the middle of the river. He ignored the command, progressing dangerously closer. He was not six feet from me when I let loose the rifle into his tree trunk of a chest. I could not believe the lack of effect. The bullets disappeared in him like fish under a wooden sea. That model Sharps, manufactured for the killing of the largest mammals on earth, was of no use against the monster. He did not flinch, nor even blink at the shot.

Before he reached me, he did thankfully change course, walking along the river instead of away from it and toward me. Welsh Widower and I gave chase along the river's edge, descending hesitantly into a dark valley, where the trees became crowded and the air heavy.

Within the shallow river valleys of Chicago, there hide undiscovered kingdoms. There, on the North Side, not two miles from my own estate on Western Avenue, sat the ruins of one. Night magic was at work there, concealing this place from the greater city which sat upon it. Thick layers of ivy accosted the old buildings and flooded the once crowded streets so thoroughly, the ruins might have been invisible to someone standing just ten feet outside of them. As I walked through the lanes, I heard furtive whispers coming from abandoned stone cottages on either side. All about me, I caught glimpses of gnarled, grimacing faces, like those within medieval paintings of infernal hell, glooming dark in the night.

Welsh Widower and I trailed our monster at a safe distance as he wandered the empty streets. We eventually made our way through a boggy courtyard and into a crumbling, plant-covered castle. We followed him as he made his way slowly through a wide, dark hall toward a dimly lit room at the far end of the castle. That room appeared to me like a royal court, with many hundred candles blazing along the walls. A good portion of the roof on one side of the room had given way, allowing the rain, which had just begun outside, to soak the floors. The monster sat on a great wooden throne, gazing down curiously at me, and I up at him.

He spoke in a hollow voice, slowly at first. The link between his mouth and his mind seemed to have diminished from years of disuse. He referred to himself by no real name, only as a "machinist." He related his past in expansive detail. I must summarize it here for the ending of this story to be understood.

***

At one time, there was a small woodland realm, which sat where the North Side of Chicago sits today. Within that place lived the machinist, only then he wasn't known as the machinist. He had an ordinary name and an ordinary life. He resided happily on the banks of what is now the North Branch of the Chicago River, within a modest stone cottage, with his wife and daughter. His wife grew vegetables in a garden. His daughter fished the river. It was a simple life, for a while.

He was a master builder and machinist, the class of which does not exist in the world today, as you will learn later in this story. Many of the machines he built were inspired by, and made for, his daughter. He made sure the girl had no want for anything. He could transform her most fantastic fantasies into realities.

One night, the machinist sat on the banks of the river, observing his daughter pirouetting on the floating river lilies in newly designed shoes of extraordinary functionality. Suddenly, the wind roared with a great storm through the woods. The machinist raced to the river's edge to save his daughter, but was too late. The water's mood changed with the weather. It claimed his daughter, sending her speeding with the current toward the lake. The machinist chased her desperately, but was no match for the river current. The girl was swept into the lake and lost.

The machinist was miserable over his lost daughter. The misery ripened over time into a mad determination: he must recover her, should it take forever. His obsession affected time for him, enabling him to somehow defy the passing of it. Those he knew died, his civilization vanished, seasons passed beyond count, yet he remained. He searched the banks of the river and the shores of the lake for an age after her disappearance, finding no trace of her.

***

After he told his tale, I respectfully offered my condolences at his unfortunate circumstances. I then related my own comparatively short history, and his place in it, particularly his scaring away of my Italian lumberjacks. He was blatantly uninterested in my grievance, gazing rudely out a glassless oriel at the thunderstorm drowning his phantom city. I regained his attention when I disclosed my designs for Riverview Amusement Park. He was captivated with certain elements of the design, notably the construction of the Ferris wheel. I would later understand why.

Claiming to be a capable engineer, he offered his services in the assembly of the Ferris wheel. I hesitantly accepted, with little hope this wandering spirit of the wood would be capable of contributing in any way to the construction of such a sophisticated machine. Our meeting concluded with my solemn promise to deliver him the architectural design documents for the Ferris wheel. In exchange for these, he gave me his own word to leave my laborers unharassed. Why he had harassed them in the first place, I never did ask.

I did not report my meeting with the machinist to anyone at the time. Should I have spoken of the matter to friends, or reported it to the proper authorities, I would have risked irreversible reputational damage, as a best-case scenario. Worst case, I'd have woken up one day a resident of Dunning Insane Asylum.

After a few days of negotiation, convincing, and the resulting higher wage, most of the Italians did return to work. The few who claimed to have encountered the machinist firsthand were the only ones to quit entirely. The gang worked satisfactorily for the duration of the task, over the course of about three weeks, completing it with no report of any monstrous presence.

The machinist's non-existence was comforting to me. After a time, I began to doubt our strange meeting had ever occurred. After all, I had never held up my end of the bargain in delivering to him the Ferris wheel architectural design documents, yet he still had not returned to haunt the Italians. Perhaps the machinist had simply been some bit of undigested dinner, a figment of my imagination as I sat dreaming by the river's edge. Surely it was possible he might have been manufactured in a dream, or in some other childish corner of my imagination.

It was just as I began to truly convince myself of this that he returned, with a Ferris wheel.

***

It sprung up noiselessly like a giant, sparkling mushroom in the night, towering above the eldest trees lining the river aside it. Hans Hasler and the rest of my soon-to-be-discharged engineering team stood staring at it, bewildered. When I inquired as to who had completed the Ferris wheel, they looked about from left to right, confused as ever. I dismissed them knowing in my heart the machinist was indeed real, and a genius beyond comprehension. He had built the Ferris wheel in two months, from nothing. It would have taken a team of the best engineers in the world two seasons at least.

I presumed the machinist would require remuneration, so thought I should find him to learn what that would be, or at least to offer my sincere appreciation. I also selfishly desired for him to teach me the means by which the wheel was powered and operated. With these objectives in mind, I ventured through the woods, following the eastward flow of the river for some time, until I happened on the familiar ruins.

My leafy-haired benefactor sat on his lonely throne, as if expecting me. I praised him for his ingenuity, going so far as to promise I would recommend his work for the most respected medals in the field of engineering. To this, he gave no response. He did, however, educate me thoroughly as to the configuration of the Ferris wheel. I was pleased to learn it was very near to being fully operational. The only thing that left me doubtful was the machine's power source. I had no means of establishing power to the wheel in short order, as my electricity did not extend so near to the river just yet. When I posed this challenge to the machinist, he said I should meet him that night at the machine for further instruction. There I met him, for the last time.

I'll not forget how swiftly the current flowed east toward the lake on that particular day. How could I? The direction of it was forever reversed by the machinist before my own eyes. You see, I believed the Ferris wheel to serve my own purposes, as any simple mind would, but the machinist intended for it a different, greater role. With it, his hope was to actually *reverse* the course of the river, pulling his daughter from the great lake that had devoured her an age prior. I believe he also made the Ferris wheel itself for her use, that she might be drawn to it, for want of a ride.

The machinist thrust a massive steel lever situated on the base of the Ferris wheel with all his might, and every bit of his might was necessary. It took him several strenuous minutes to get the lever entirely moved. I don't believe there is a force on earth that could move that lever in the opposite direction, and it has remained in the position he left it that day. The lever jerked the Ferris wheel into motion, causing an eerie moan of resistance from within the depths of the river. The waters halted their flow entirely, gurgling as if confused. After a short minute, the waters miraculously changed course, flowing swiftly west, toward the Mississippi, when mere seconds earlier they had flowed east, toward Lake Michigan. And the Ferris wheel spun round.

There, for the first time, I saw the machinist smile. His teeth looked like saplings.

***

As you now know, Riverview Amusement Park has been a smashing success, far grander than my original aspirations. It is the world's largest amusement park, covering seventy-four acres between Belmont and Western Avenues. The Ferris wheel is still there, circling children about the city sky. From the highest heights, they gaze down at the enchanted river and are made to feel enchanted themselves.

The river continues to flow in reverse. The Sanitary Engineers Corps promptly took credit for changing its course, going so far as to claim they had reversed the river to mitigate the possibility of another waterborne cholera epidemic (caused in 1885, when sewage from the river ran off into the Lake Michigan drinking-water supply). Their so-called project was hailed as a public works wonder. It is still considered one of the most brilliant engineering achievements of its time.

It never happened.

As for the machinist, there is little more to say. I never

learned if he retrieved his daughter. I have not seen him in the woodsy flesh since that day on the river. He is real now only as I sleep in the night, bursting forth through cobwebs of fast-fading memories, to the shores of Lake Michigan, where he wanders beneath my own window in his everlasting lament.

The city is no longer the untamed child she was in those early days of Riverview. She's outgrown simple, celestial pleasures, and sadly, so have I. I hardly remember the boy I once was. He has been swallowed in a sea of the tedious, toiling years that have since passed. The sight of the Ferris wheel helps me to remember him. I think that is why I find myself lurking about the grounds there so often—perhaps I'll encounter the machinist. If he can change the course of a river, surely he can grant me the joy of a boy catching raindrops on his tongue.

We all got lost in the woods as children

Cowboys and Indians

"What'll happen if the Ferris wheel is torn down?" Rich asked. "Will the river turn back around?"

The old man didn't say anything at first. He was exhausted from telling his story. Only after another spin of the Ferris wheel did he respond in a sad whisper, and more slowly than before.

"First, not *if* it will be torn down, but *when*. Second, regarding the river, I don't know what will happen, but I think nothing. I believe it would take the machinist himself to change the course of it once more. I think, when someday this Ferris wheel is no more, and even when this park is gone, the river will continue to flow in reverse, and no one will remember the river when it flowed any other way. And no one will remember Riverview."

The old man's face turned twisted and sad. It was as though he'd never pondered the future of his life's work beyond his own lifetime. The Ferris wheel's behavior changed with his mood; it began to speed up, slowly at first, then when the old man started sobbing in his hands, it turned even faster, and the harder he sobbed, the faster it spun. Just when it seemed they might all be thrown from their seats, Francesca put her hand in the old man's, and the Ferris wheel slowed, until it finally came to a halt. Their carriage stopped at a high point, as high on the wheel as they could be.

The old man stood slowly. He looked down into the river, then to the forest, then back to the river. He stepped onto the thin lip of the carriage. The wind held him up, ruffling his gray hair.

"When I die, I hope not for heaven, hell, or oblivion. No. I would not care for those places at all," he said. "When I die, I hope to be the ghost of the Gravitron. It is my favorite ride. I have not ridden it since I could, since I was young. I wish I could spin and spin and spin, for all the duration of time. I hope there is a place for amusement parks to go when they are no more, so I can be the ghost of the Gravitron there as well. I hope for nothing more than that."

The old man stood silently for a few seconds, then disappeared with a sprightly leap off the ledge of the carriage, falling toward the river. He struck the water with a horrendous slap. Rich gasped, too shocked to scream. He gasped again when he looked down. Within the dark river, he saw the white head of the old man. He was bobbing like a buoy, kicking his legs, rowing his arms in the water, flowing swiftly with the current, away from the city. Rich thought he heard the old man actually *singing*: "The west wind doth blow, and soon it will snow."

The Ferris wheel spun around once more before letting them off. They ran to the riverside for some sign of the old man, but found none.

***

The bizarre encounter struck Rich as a sign they should leave Riverview. But where would they go? Most of the park was surrounded by woods. The Lavender Line seemed the only way out.

"When does the Lavender Line pick up again?" Rich asked Francesca.

"No more pickups tonight, Rich, not here at Riverview at least. Don't worry, though, I know a shortcut to get where we're going."

"A shortcut to where, exactly?"

"We're taking a shortcut to the Green Mill, where we'll go for the music inside, to settle your nervous nerves. You look awful! We can cut through those woods over to the Lavender Line stop at Rhine Falls. Won't take more than a few minutes of walking. A stroll through the woods will help calm you down."

She grabbed hold of Rich's hand, and they started toward the woods. The forest was nearly pitch black. All Rich could see between the trees were scattered pillars of moonlight shining through chinks in the leaves above.

Before they reached the forest, Rich asked Francesca the same question he had asked when he'd first caught her, during that game of ghost in the graveyard. Then, she had given him only a name. He wanted to learn more, if he could.

"Who are you again?"

"I told you, it's Francesca. Well, Francesca Finnegan is

my name, though I can't remember who gave it to me, or when I got it. I've always felt like Wendy Darling, had she run out of fairy dust on her way to spring cleaning in Neverland, and ended up splashing down into Belmont Harbor. What does it matter, though? You'll forget me when the city has turned old for you, but I'll still be here, because it won't be old for everyone." Despite what Francesca said, she might have been described in simpler terms: if Peter Pan was the boy who refused to grow up, she was the girl who refused.

"Where are you from?"

"Who knows? Maybe from a tear in the flesh of the city, ripped out by the teeth of a Jabberwock, at the intersection of something here and something there, right where you stop believing in last—"

Francesca was interrupted by a POP POP POP of gunfire from within the forest. She and Rich ran and hid behind a wide tree, each peering out from around the opposite side of it. A violent scene unfolded before them.

A short distance into the woods, two silhouettes chased each other through the trees, sometimes stopping for a second to shoot, but mostly running and screaming. The sound and light from the gunshots made the two easy to follow in the darkness. Rich could see that the man in pursuit was dressed something like a cowboy. The other man looked like an Indian.

"Cowboys and Indians," Rich thought.

The chase soon came uncomfortably near to Francesca and Rich, with the Indian stopping to reload his pistol not fifteen feet from where they hid. The Indian turned to shoot at his attacker, who was then running faster than ever, closing the gap between them. The cowboy didn't hide at all from the Indian's shots, which must have missed him. The Indian then dropped his gun and pulled a tomahawk from his waistband, breathing in drawn-out, labored gasps, waiting for the fight to come to him. And it did. The cowboy was on him in seconds. The Indian raised his arm to strike down his enemy, but was too slow. The cowboy drew his pistol so fast, Rich saw nothing of the act but gun smoke. The cowboy had fired a single shot through the Indian, who slumped over against a tree, as if taking a nap.

Rich lost his head at the sight of the dead Indian and fell clumsily out from behind the tree they hid behind, landing squarely on his back. The cowboy looked at Rich, then at Francesca. He didn't appear the least bit startled. With a handkerchief, he carefully cleaned the Indian's blood from his gun and face, then made his way toward them.

"Two guttersnipes! Whatever are you doing out here in the wild? Where do you come from? Were you a captive of the red man? His spirit is off to the happy hunting grounds."

Francesca stepped forward. "No, sir, we are on our own. We are Riverview Park-goers taking a shortcut toward the Green Mill."

"You are looking for a green *what*? A mill? I give that tale no credence. You are in Illinois, and that means wilderness. This forest is more virgin than the Virgin Mary. You will not find a mill of any kind for some ways. The Fort Dearborn not far from where we stand has been butchered and burned and blackened by the Potawatomi tribe of our newly dead friend here. You ought to deliver yourselves to the Grand Duke at Rhine Falls and catch the Lavender Line to somewhere else."

Francesca's voice rose in anger. "I give you no credence! The Green Mill isn't a place for grinding grain. It's a jazz club and pub, in the city. We do intend to catch the Lavender Line at Rhine Falls, which will take us to the Green Mill."

"Well, aren't you the curly wolf with your hair like water, and your pubs and clubs. The first of the frontier-town bars, is it? Listen to me, once and good. The only spit-and-sawdust near here is within Fort Wayne. And you may be disappointed with the place. It is no jubilee. The beer in Fort Wayne tastes like curds and whey."

"We *are* going to the Green Mill. We *are* taking a shortcut through these woods to the Lavender Line stop at Rhine Falls, which *you*, sir, have clearly never ridden, or you would know better. Fort Wayne is not our concern, and neither are *you*." Francesca was almost yelling at the man, who still held a gun in his hand, and had fresh blood on his shirt.

Rich of course hoped Francesca would stop arguing.

The man turned to Rich. Rich tried not to stare at the long scar on his face, which began at the corner of his left eye, widening and deepening as it ran down his thin cheek, ending at his jaw line. The rest of the man's face was gritty, in contrast to his expressive eyes. He wore animal furs, leather moccasins, and an open-crown hat. Rich didn't know what to think of him.

"Boy, you look all green about the gills. Do not be afraid. I mean you no harm, though I dare not speak for your friend here. She is not of delicate temperament. Lucky for you, I am in a generous way today. I will extend an offer to you two lost children. I will allow you to follow me. But beware! The path we travel to get there is not the safest. I am tracking the last of the Potawatomi in order to kill every single brave."

"In what direction are you headed, and what is your name?" Francesca asked.

"I go east, toward the great lake. I will pass your Rhine Falls. They call me John Kinzie, formerly the fur trader of Quebec. I have no middle name."

"John Kinzie. I know your name. I know of a street called Kinzie," Francesca thought aloud.

"You know of nothing called Kinzie, but I can guess at the yarns you heard spun about me. Did you hear that I murdered Jean La Lime in Fort Dearborn and fled north to join with an Indian federation? Maybe I am even a chief by now? Well, here is me in the flesh. That which you hear is untrue."

"I've heard all kinds of untruths. There are more untruths than truths."

"Sure there are. Follow me while I tell you truths."

"We'll follow you as far as we need."

"Into the trees with us all, then."

The three started into the forest. It swallowed them, as only a great forest can.

Defense by Henry Herring, 1928. The sculpture is located on the wall of a bridge tender's house on Michigan Avenue Bridge.

The Polish Potawatomi

And a great forest it was. It was a real forest, much different from the city forests Rich was used to. City forests aren't really forests at all, they're more like groves, or pitiful little patches of trees labeled "forest preserve." Forest preserves are filled with passing headlights, trash, and the mechanical clatter of the city. They contain few actual woodland creatures, except for the odd squirrel, bloated on trash. You'll find the occasional Wicca or homeless crowd in a forest preserve, but that's about it. Definitely no fur traders or Indians. And forest preserves are not capable of swallowing, or getting lost in, as this forest was.

This forest was an enclosure. Once inside, there was no proof of outside. The only evidence of anything other than the forest was the occasional patch of moonlight, but those appeared less and less as Francesca, Rich, and Kinzie made their way deeper into the heart of the woods. The trees were thick and crowded, and the path the three walked was narrow and overgrown with roots. The swoosh of leaves above was so loud that at times, it was hard to make any conversation at all. But Rich didn't mind that. As you know, he liked the wind.

Francesca led the way, skipping backward along the trail, twisting and turning without facing forward, as though she knew the way by heart, or had eyes in the back of her head. She faced Kinzie, peppering him with questions. He gave mostly quiet, laconic replies. Only one question led to any real conversation.

"Mr. Kinzie, you said you would tell us truths! So tell us, where did you get that big, ugly scar on your face?"

"The story of that scar is the story of a fight. It was Fort Dearborn which caused it."

"You said Fort Dearborn was burned down. Was there a battle? You absolutely *must* tell us a story of the battle. Battle stories make for great walking stories. And a city battle story is the best battle story of all."

"My own remembrance of that 'battle' is clear as white lightning. The years that have passed, on the other hand, those are murky. I lost count when I lost count of them. When the 'battle' occurred, I was a boy barely seventeen, who had not yet kissed a girl. It was the year of our lord one thousand seventeen hundred and something. Me and a compatriot by the curious name of Hardik the Hindu were fixing to French-leave the damned Fort. Our idea was to absquatulate like phantoms. That was the plan, at least. It didn't happen that way."

"What does absquatulate mean?" Rich cut in. Kinzie's speech was at times difficult for Rich to understand. It was uneducated, yet intelligent, from somewhere well outside the city.

Kinzie ignored the question.

"Before you learn the story of the Dearborn Massacre you must learn the story of the Potawatomi tribe who hunt the Illinois Territory. The Potawatomi had a Slav as chief, if you can believe that. Still do, as I hear it said. It is the most unusual thing to see a group of Indians following a 'white eye.' He had less Indian blood than you or me, by the look of him. His own eyes were blue as a funeral, below a head of bushy blond hair. You could tell straight away he was not native. I did not trust the man from the start, and he likewise.

"I met him on many an occasion, because we traded with the Indians here and there, mostly watery whiskey for skins and seeds. It was a mutually beneficial arrangement. Somewhere in that time Hardik named him Polish Potawatomi, on account of his Slavic features. Hardik the Hindu was the cleverest of us all. I feel less thoughtful without his witfulness about."

Kinzie stopped suddenly. "Excuse me, I must have a moment," he said. He then had a moment, which meant stopping to piss directly in front of them. "You must not venture too far off the path," he explained. They walked on.

"As I was saying—for a time, relations with the Potawatomi were civilized. In the coldest winters we harbored their sick young braves, and I could not have imagined the end result of the whole relationship would be as it would be. I even took a fancy to a squaw, though she would not look me in the eye. I think she and the other Potawatomi thought I was a ghost, what with the way I'm always so pale. I heard once the Indians treated freckles as a corruption, or a deformity of the spirit. If that's true, they must have considered my spirit excessively deformed. My skin is swarmed with freckles in the summer months. All the same, the squaw danced a rain dance for me in the night, in my dreams. And that is more than nothing, is it not? A dream is more than nothing."

Kinzie looked back at Rich, who quickly nodded in agreement.

"It was around this time that Chicago got her name from the Indian word shikaakwa, which means smelly onion," Kinzie explained.

"BULLLLL *shit*," Francesca interrupted. "Chicago is an acronym. CHICAGO. It means **C**hicago **H**as **I**mps, **C**ab fares, **A**nd **G**argantuan **O**wlbears. Everyone knows that! It's common knowledge, common as the fact the shit-eating pigeons of Daley Plaza are all reincarnated investment bankers."

Rich wondered if it were possible for an acronym to be within an acronym, as Kinzie continued.

"Whatever you say little girl. Now, as for the 'battle.' Things went sour with the Potawatomi so fast, I don't remember the original cause. I think it had to do with the newly declared war between the empires of France and Britain. The Potawatomi found themselves on the French side of it for whatever reason. I don't recall why. It's probable a sly Frenchman guaranteed them a flood's worth of some stale brandy. The Indians could be easily bought that way. I saw an Indian once trade a horse for a single pint of stout. They use liquor to cure everything from snakebites to scabies. If the Indians are ever learned in the brewing arts, they will drink themselves to extinction and be cured of all affliction, at the same time.

"On account of the proximate French and Indian dangers posed to our Fort Dearborn, the whole garrison was ordered to evacuate eastward to Fort somewhere. I forget where. We left old Dearborn about midday, on a strange day of green skies and fishy lake wind. We were led by one Captain William Wells. There were no more than a hundred of us. Half that amount were armed redcoat regulars, the other half women and children. We walked in a slow, single-file order down the king's road until we reached the great lake, at which point we walked along the sand dunes, keeping the lake to our side as we moved east. We could not have been more than three miles from the fort, when one of our scouts reported no fewer than five hundred braves clustered behind a high sand dune, just ahead, all drenched in war paint and fucked to hell on whiskey. It was then I knew, the strange day was to get stranger.

"Myself, Hardik, and several others rushed up the dunes at the Indians. You may think that illogical, and I would not blame you for it. It turned out to be, but our hope was that the sudden onslaught might panic the Indians, or cause them to run away. Neither occurred. Instead, the Indians trampled over us in a demented fury. Our charge had no effect but to divide us, allowing a separate group of fiends led by the Polish Potawatomi to murder all we'd left behind. I tumbled back down the dune, where I saw the error in our strategy. It was a view of damnation. The first sight I saw was a dead boy like a mangled marionette, the assassin upon his mother a few feet away. I shot that particular Indian until he was dead, twice over. Looking up, over some ways, I saw a circle of Indians sharing in an unusual feast, the entree being the gushing heart of Captain Wells. I hear some Indians believe to eat a man's heart is to inherit his courage, and this is why they devoured the heart, easy as dessert. Only Wells was no lion, so I expect it did them no good.

"With the slaughter all around, I guessed in my head I would soon be dead. Given that eventuality, gutting the Polish Potawatomi struck me as a suitable final course of action. I observed him on his white mare, riding about in conquest like a horseman of the apocalypse, overseeing this or that butchery, not far from me. He wore a proud grin, the quality of which would have made the Devil wish he had it. He smiled it at me, and I knew then I must send him to his maker. It felt the purpose of my being.

"When I ran his way, his infernal grin dissolved. I did not have the patience to reload my cavalry pistol. I ran at him with fists clenched, intending to beat him into the arms of his great spirit. He turned his horse and dashed off into the woods a short way inland, toward the edge of a river. Once there, he dismounted and turned to engage me with a timber club in hand. Hard to say why he didn't simply shoot me. That was a mistake on his part.

"To my dismay, he was skilled with the club. The fact he had a weapon at all also helped his situation, though I think he could have beat me without it. He was stronger and faster than most, and I was not in sporting condition that day. I had been getting over a winter disease of the native sort, so was skinny and weak. It was therefore not hard for him to club me within an inch of my life on the river's edge, gifting me with the scar on my face, the one you noticed. It is only for Hardik the Hindu that I am alive today.

"I do not know wherever Hardik came from. I'd lost track of him after our foolish charge up the dunes. He surprised not only myself, but also the Polish Potawatomi. Hardik came down on him with a wrath, cutlass in hand, forcing him back into the river, where the two fought for some time, as I lay bleeding, helpless on the riverside. Their clash was like that of Saint Michael waging battle upon Lucifer. That is to say, it looked unnatural. The wretched Indian's blood glowed green like the flash of first sun in the morning, or the last at dusk. It stained the whole of the river, so you could almost mistake it for a grass path.

"The fight went on in the river of green. The Polish Potawatomi and Hardik the Hindu were an even match. I could not tell which way things would go, when something most unexpected happened. A thick mist from the forest invaded the river, overtaking them like I seen the tide overtake sand. Last I saw, before they were consumed, they were wrestling about in a deeper part of the river. They disappeared then in the mist. I have seen neither since.

"There is my account of the Battle of Fort Dearborn, and the tale of the Polish Potawatomi, unusual as it may sound. I have been looking to deliver justice on the tribe since that day."

***

"The city has more Polish than Poland," Francesca said. "Where do you expect to find the Polish Potawatomi?"

"He was last spotted on the lakeshore after the Treaty of Chicago was agreed. At the concluding ceremony for the treaty, a band of braves led by him gathered atop a great dune, around a tall fire. In full dress, and brandishing instruments of battle, they danced the last official war dance within the city limits, but I think they still dance it on the unofficial. I think I will find them near the lakeshore dancing a dance, one day."

The three walked on in silence. The trail began to slope upward, slightly at first, then steeper. Rich soon grew tired. He felt as though they were no longer walking in a forest, but scaling a tree-covered mountain. The steepness of the path slowed them all considerably.

Kinzie looked at Rich and Francesca. "I have told you something of my history. Will you not tell me something of your own? It will quicken the walk."

Francesca shrugged her shoulders. "My history is magic and machinists. Rich's history is less interesting."

"Magic. I have never been one to believe in the magic. Tell me of the magic."

"Well, you wouldn't know magic, now would you? That's because there is typically no magic in a man, though you've seen a tad yourself, what with the river of green. This forest itself is magic, as is the Lavender Line. Riverview is magic. The Polish Potawatomi may have some magic in him. But magic's place in your history is of no consequence, because the author of that history is a businessman like our Rich here will someday be. The businessman is a censor of magic. Rich will call himself Richard and be a businessman of business, won't you, Rich? Richard the simple, surly vice president of something is what they'll call you."

"Sure." Rich was too out of breath to object. Kinzie looked back at him with some concern.

"Your businessman of business is played out. His face looks hot as a whorehouse on nickel night. But I agree, the Lavender Line is most peculiar. I do not ride it. It is like a phantasm. I hear a witch drives it. Tell me, what of things that are not magic. What of things that are real?"

"The things that are real make no difference to me. One single second of a single dream is far more interesting to me than a lifetime of reality, because in that second I'd know if I really cared to, I could fly."

"What about a businessman of business? What type of man is that? I have not heard of a man like that. He is not magic?"

"No. A businessman of business is a slave who sits all day in a confined space, where he performs tasks assigned to him by a slave master. The slave master is another businessman, who reports to his own slave master of business. The tasks assigned by the slave master hierarchy rarely require the businessman to stand up or go outside, so he eventually becomes fat and disgusting and sick. Businessmen take a slave ship called the L to work every day. Businessmen hope for nothing more than to move higher and higher on the pyramid of slave masters, so as to reduce the amount of slave labor they themselves have to perform. Businessmen encourage their children to be like-minded slaves. Businessmen are forgotten almost the moment they die. They leave nothing behind but numbers within a bank account and the occasional Toyota Camry, because what will an old widow do with two cars?"

Kinzie shook his head in disgust. "Who would desire to be such a man?"

***

They'd been climbing steadily for some time, when, to Rich's relief, they reached a flat, grassy ridge. Relief turned to disbelief as he looked down through the trees and saw they were on the edge of a wide, tree-filled valley. There was a break in the trees at the lowest point, where a rough, winding river flowed into a waterfall. The splash of rapids echoed unmistakably through the night. A small, square, white-stone citadel, like a castle keep without a castle, three stories high, with a turret on each of its four corners, stood alone within a calm pool of water, not far from the base of the waterfall. A skinny pier stretched from the shore to the keep.

"Behold Rhine Falls!" Kinzie said. "Nab your tickets for the Lavender Line from the grand duke in there. I will accompany you down that way, then must be on my own way."

They followed Kinzie down a wooden staircase, spiraling through pine trees, deeper into the valley. Rich didn't know what to think of a waterfall in the city, but then he didn't know what to think of any of what he'd seen since he'd jumped after Francesca into the river. So he followed Kinzie and Francesca quietly, as if this were all part of an ordinary Friday night.

After a while, they found themselves facing the keep on the water, from the edge of the skinny pier leading toward it. The keep looked dark and empty. There was no sign of anyone inside.

"The grand duke holds court on the third floor." Kinzie pointed. "Up there. Look!"

As if in answer to Kinzie's gesture, the spidery shadow of a man suddenly formed within a third-story window, in a glow of firelight. Rich saw a little orange spark burning from within the base of the man's huge smoking pipe. Trails of thick smoke journeyed from the pipe, out the window, up into space.

"Give the duke my fondest. I must be away now. Goodbye, little girl, goodbye, businessman. May you get home safe and sound, wherever that may be! If you see a Potawatomi squaw, remember me to her. Last I saw her, she was standing all alone in a glade, praying to daisies."

Kinzie turned away, starting up into the trees.

"Won't you take a ride on the Lavender Line yourself?" Francesca asked Kinzie, as he walked away. "There is a train arrives every hour on the hour. It goes in the direction of the lake. You can sit with us, if you like."

Kinzie stopped, standing still for a moment as if in thought, then turned around. "Did you not say there was no magic in a man?"

He wasn't wrong.

Sir, there is ash in your mustache

The Grand Duke of Rhine Falls

Rich and Francesca walked carefully over the water, along the rickety wood pier toward the keep. They came to a rotted door held upright by a single surviving hinge. The door swung wildly in the wind, like underwear on a clothesline. Rich held it in place for Francesca as she walked in.

"Danke," she said. Rich wondered what that meant.

The first floor of the place looked like it was once a restaurant. Empty tables and chairs, covered in thick layers of snow-white dust, were strewn everywhere. It looked as if the restaurant had been quickly and permanently abandoned years ago, after some ruckus. Francesca and Rich walked through the dining room toward a circular stone stairwell within the opposite wall, where they made their way up to the third floor.

The third floor was as rich as Richard himself would someday be, much different from the first floor. Rich found himself standing on Persian carpet within a comfortable stone chamber of high, intricately carved wooden beamed ceilings, where everything glowed red from a bonfire blazing inside an enormous brick fireplace. The walls were decorated with dozens of elegant Victorian paintings. A large map of curious markings hung above the fireplace. A long stone bar stood along the wall opposite the stairwell. There were luxurious furnishings everywhere. Rich guessed from the room that the grand duke was someone of importance, someone royal.

The grand duke sat hunched over a small wooden coffee table, near the open window where they'd observed his shadow from below. He was smoking a gigantic corncob pipe, the chamber so big it looked more like a coffee mug than anything intended for smoking. The grand duke himself appeared nearly as extraordinary as his pipe. He was neither young nor old, not royal, but not altogether common. His style was the embodiment of that old, *old-*fashioned masculinity, which matched the room. He wore an impeccable navy blue three-piece suit, complete with top hat and time piece. He was a skinny man, with a jet-black wax mustache, which hid his mouth entirely. His left eye had a cast that made it seem as if he were looking beyond you. Rich had never seen such a man, or mustache.

The grand duke greeted them enthusiastically. It was evident he and Francesca already knew each other. He hugged Francesca, then shook Rich's hand with a painful, bone-cracking squeeze.

"Guten tag! Was möchten zee trinken?" He offered a drink to them, in his native German.

"Yes sie bitte," Francesca replied. "I will take three teaspoons of powdered sugar within three measures of Malört, below two measures of tap water and a measure of

Moxie soda. Stir it for one second, or until the powder looks like milk, then add a stem of some sort. Oh, and I'll take that in a brandy balloon, if you have it. It is the only proper way to drink Malört in society."

"Zee usual, yes, ma'am." The grand duke switched from German to English, with the heaviest of accents. He looked to Rich for his drink.

"Sir?"

"A beer?" Sounded safe to Rich.

"I vill get you zee hoppiest in zee house." Rich didn't understand what the man meant by "hoppiest." Rich wouldn't come to appreciate the flavor of hops for years, and the accent made the grand duke's utterances all the more confusing.

Francesca and Rich sat next to each other on a leather sofa in front of the fire, while the duke tended to drinks behind the bar.

"I notice you ver led here by Kinzie. He is zee restless shpirit, is he not? Will shtay zat vay until he finds zee blue-eyed Indian. He zinks zee Indian chief is so different from him, but zay are not zat different. Under efery brown eye is a blue eye. Zee only difference between a brown eye and a blue eye is a thin layer of pigment on zee surface."

Francesca nodded. "Agreed. Kinzie says to give you his fondest regards. I didn't know you two knew each other, seeing as he doesn't ride the Lavender Line. How long have you known him?"

The grand duke gazed toward the ceiling in thought. "I don't remember efer not knowing Kinzie. He vas here before zee Lafender Line laid tracks, and I expect he'll be here ven zee last train runs. I see less of him lately. He shtops in for a pipe of cavendish or a vitefish now and zen, zat's about it."

The grand duke served the drinks, then sat on the sofa across from them, puffing on his supreme corncob pipe, blowing rings of smoke into the fire. The tobacco was flavored with cherry skin, and Rich loved the smell of the smoke. It was a smell Rich wished he could take home with him. He smiled at the smell as he stared at the curious map above the fireplace. The map was unlike anything he'd seen, and it contained (he thought) nowhere he'd been. There were ghosts, elves, fairies, forests, mountains, rivers, and castles. A dotted Lavender Line wound this way and that through the map.

The grand duke detected Rich's interest. "Boy, you haf zee look of a cartographer. Vat do you zink of zee map zere? I drew it myself."

"I like it, but, I mean—I guess I don't know what to make of it. It's not anywhere I've been, as far as I can tell. It's nowhere I've seen. I'd like to know where the places on the map are. What's this a map *of?*"

"Vye, don't you see, zis is a map of zee places you haf been, zee places you might go, and zee place you are now. Zee dotted line zere is zee path of zee Lafender Line." The grand duke stood up and pointed to a clump of trees on the map. "You are exactly here, just outside of Schaffhausen, at zee Rhine Falls. You came from here." He pointed to a Ferris wheel. "Do not get lost, you could end up in Germany or Svitzerland or Roseland! Haha."

"Never heard of Schaffhausen. That a suburb or something? How do you get there? And how did we get from there to here?"

"Haha! Asking how to get anyvere on zis map is like asking vere to fall down a rabbit hole, or how to valk srough a looking glass. If you opened a compass right now, it vould ask you for directions north. Zee Lafender Line trafels a shpan of area beyond vat you vould expect from an ordinary train. It crosses zee ramparts vithin zee var between zee boy you are and zee man you vill be, zee clash between young and old. Dance your fairy dance vith Frankie vile you may, zere is a point beyond vich she, me, and zee Lafender Line vill be inaccessible to you."

Rich walked up to the map and pointed to a great castle, next to a splash of bright green paint. "What's this castle here?"

"It is zee castle of zee Kingdom of Aragon. It is most beautiful under zee shtars. Zere is a ball zere tonight." The grand duke looked at Francesca. "I trust you vill attend, m'lady."

"Of course I'll attend. Richard the rich here is my date! We plan to go to the Green Mill before, just for a drink."

"Ah yes, zee mill of Green. Zee Lafender Line vill haf you zere in no time."

The three relaxed around the fire. When a cold draft blew in through the window, accompanied by a few errant snowflakes, the grand duke draped Francesca in a furry blanket from behind the bar to keep her warm. She was content to sip from her drink and stare quietly into the flames. Rich and the grand duke continued discussing this or that feature of the map, until Rich had exhausted his curiosity, and sat back down next to Francesca. The grand duke settled into his little table by the window, where he repacked his pipe, lighting it with a large torch from the wall. He hummed a song as he sat smoking:

Rich and Frankie in zee night
Upon zee Ferris wheel take flight
Rich and Frankie ride zee Lafender
To zee Green Mill zay meander

***

"We must be going, Rich," Francesca announced after a while. "Grand duke, you are the most royal of hosts. We hope to see you at the castle ball."

Whether it was the tone in her voice or her sudden sense of urgency, for the first time, it struck Rich there was some ending to the night, and it was not far away. He wondered how nights like this ended, and if the endings were as unexpected as the beginnings.

The grand duke said goodbye as he had said hello, hugging Francesca and giving Rich's hand that same murderous handshake. "Valk back to zee pier. Zere vill be a rowboat vaiting. Row srough zee vaterfall to zee Lafender."

The grand duke returned to his little table, where he sat comfortably with his feet propped up on the windowsill, blowing smoke into the night sky. Before Rich followed Frankie down the stairs, he glanced back over his shoulder for a last sniff of the cherry tobacco, but to his surprise, there was no sign of the grand duke. There was nothing left of him but the cloudy remnants of smoke, sailing out the window up into the night.

Outside, Rich was surprised at how much warmer it suddenly felt. A little white rowboat was floating where the grand duke said it would be. Rich declared he must row it, in a chivalrous sort of way. The problem with Rich rowing the boat was that Rich had never rowed a boat, so he was not very good at rowing a boat. He worked his skinny arms to exhaustion in only a few minutes, causing the boat to drift and wobble awkwardly toward the base of the waterfall.

Francesca didn't mind the slow going. She was secretly humored by Rich's clumsy attempt at the rowing, and besides, the stars were out in masses. If Rich had stopped rowing and taken a second to look closely into the waters, he would have observed the water sprites dancing wildly in reflection of the stars.

It took many minutes of huffing and puffing for Rich to cover the short distance from the shore to the base of the waterfall. By the time they finally reached it, Rich was drenched from head to toe in sweat. He welcomed the cool shower from the thin curtain of the waterfall, which covered him completely as he rowed through it. Francesca reached under her seat for a conveniently placed umbrella and opened it above her head to stay dry.

Hidden behind the waterfall was a large cavern, like a mineshaft, not unlike the one where they'd first caught the Lavender Line. They docked the boat and stood together, waiting again for the train. Rich commented on the similarities between that first stop and this one. Francesca explained the reason.

"The Lavender Line stops should look the same. Long ago, each of the stops was part of a single cable-car network. Miles and miles of cable car ran deep below the city surface, carrying city-goers, until the dreaded L debuted, and it closed. The official story you'll hear is that the cable-car tunnels have been sealed since then, but as you can see, that is untrue. The Lavender Line runs through the old cable-car tunnels, with no one above to notice or care."

In a few minutes, they heard the familiar shriek of the Lavender Line whistle. A Bengal-cat conductor led Francesca swiftly and delicately up into the train, with Rich following close behind. They didn't walk into any of the main passenger cars. Instead, they stood in that limbo between the passenger car and the exit doors.

"We're only one stop away," Francesca reasoned.

The ride was a short rumbling up a steep grade. Francesca explained to Rich that the cable-car grade of the past was four times as steep as that of the L today. The train let them out in another cavern, this one with stairs leading up and outside, into an alley, where the rain was pouring down.

Francesca grabbed hold of Rich's hand and led him splashing and laughing through the alley's center drain. The rain fell from the sky and up from puddles and in through the side, when the wind rose. The rain covered Rich's face and seeped in his mouth and dripped down his throat. It tasted sweet as soda, and when Rich swallowed it, he was positive he'd live forever. It was the second-to-last time rain would make him feel like that.

They turned a corner and found themselves suddenly standing in front of the Green Mill, in Uptown. Rich was somewhat relieved to be in a recognizable part of the city again, though he hoped for more adventures with Francesca. He hoped for another ride on the Lavender Line.

Above them, the light from the stars faded, hidden beneath a veil of purple. The Green Mill's kelly-green marquee shone against the not-so-dark sky, and Rich wondered why. Why was the sky above the city only as black as violet and not some darker shade? Scientists called it light pollution, and while that might have been true elsewhere, it was not the case in Chicago.

No, the city's nightly nightlight could be traced to the Green Mill Cocktail Lounge.

Rain on Broadway and Lawrence, Uptown

The Green Mill Breaks Through

Long ago, the Green Mill struggled to survive. The ale was stale, the electric marquee blinked a pale cry for help, and lonely nights passed without a single patron's sip of Southside. If nothing had changed, the place would soon have been bankrupted and abandoned. Luckily, something did change.

One afternoon, around the time the Green Mill was at its worst, the owner busied himself behind the red oak bar, nervously cleaning the already sparkling steel exterior of the cash register, wishing he could make use of it. An extraordinary customer interrupted him.

She wore a high moss-colored stovepipe hat and a riding habit, which made her look like a lost circus ringmaster. She paused in the doorway, her eyes searching the empty bar from side to side, top to bottom. She asked in a desperately hopeful tone, "Have you seen my daughter, Francesca Finnegan? She has slapped cheeks beneath a blue head of hair. She stood no taller than your barstools here last I saw her."

The owner told her no, unfortunately he had not seen a girl fitting that description in the neighborhood. "But are you thirsty, madam? I'll happily pour a refreshment on the house." It was the least he could do. The woman sauntered up to the bar and ordered what she called a grassy bourbon, an even mixture of Kentucky bourbon and Green River soda. When mixed, the concoction turned a hazel that matched the woman's eyes. She took one sip and then, as if startled by the silence, asked why she was the bar's lone customer.

The owner explained that the emptiness was typical, and that he would be forced to close soon on account of it. The woman pondered his response, then placed her hat on the bar, revealing long silver hair that disagreed with her young complexion. She saw herself in the mirror behind the bar and examined her reflection curiously, as if she were seeing it for the first time. When the owner turned his back to her, continuing his nervous polishing of the cash register, she locked eyes with him in the mirror and made an unusual proposition.

"You call this hovel the Green Mill, but the place is more blue than green—in fact, my hat here is greener. I'll give you green, and with it that fortune you smartly bet on when you first thought of this place. I'll have you know, green draws crowds. Double your liquor stores and you'll still be drunk dry nightly. Lines of Chicagoans stretching miles west down Lawrence Avenue will wait into the night for a slight chance to hear one single note from the jazz band. The founding fathers of blues will beg you to let them play on that pitiful wood plank you call a stage. And you will be great yourself. This city will know you. With green, that is."

The owner thought the woman sounded sincere, but misunderstood the offer. He figured her an eccentric moneylender, and the green to which she referred of course a loan. The woman continued, as if reading his mind.

"You mistake me for a financier! I'd have guessed the Devil. No, I've not sold money, not once. The green I recommend doesn't come in the form of a bank note. I meant the color green alone. You require it in that pale-yellow, piss-colored electric marquee outside. The marquee should be green, and the source of the green is every bit as important as the color itself. Where will we get it, you wonder? The answer is above us. We'll blend the black of the Midwestern night sky with that disgraceful yellow. The mixture should produce a kelly green that will burn beautiful as ever!"

The owner felt doubtful. He doubted both the credibility of the offer and his ability to reciprocate. He had very little to give her in return. Once again, he didn't have to voice his concerns before she addressed them.

"Have you heard of a cabaret in Paris called the Moulin Rouge? The English translation of that cabaret's name is Red Mill, and it has been red (and renowned) only since my last visit. Believe me, this deal is no less mysterious than the Red Line's running under the Chicago River."

She paused, confirming the owner's newly gained trust. "As for terms, this is no Faustian pact. Your soul can't find my daughter for me. However, a lighter sky can. Transferring a shade of midnight into your sign outside is to our mutual benefit. It will turn your sign green and lighten the night for me. It is impossible to find my daughter in this darkness."

She had only one other term: if the owner recognized her daughter, he should turn the green marquee off as a signal to her that the girl had been found.

The owner agreed.

The next night, a rare dry lightning storm passed low over the city. There wasn't a drop of rain, though the lightning strikes and severe winds loomed constantly. In the early-morning hours, a downdraft struck the Green Mill, changing the color of the exterior bar sign from yellow to green. Later that night, the storm clouds broke over Lake Michigan and revealed a sky that should have been darker.

***

The evenings above the city remain an elderly twilight, stranded between dusk and darkness. The Green Mill still sits on Lawrence and Broadway, marquee lit, one of the busiest bars in the city. The woman was last seen on the far South Side of Chicago, wandering the shores of Rainbow Beach, looking for her daughter.

The Green Mill's owner of course did meet Francesca Finnegan one day. He just didn't turn off the green marquee. Why would he?

He was a businessman.

Lucy Leather Legs

The Sad Chapter

Rich thought of his own father, who'd been dead only a few years, as he and Francesca walked toward the Green Mill. Bars reminded Rich of his father because his father had practically lived in them. Rich's first father-son memory took place in a bar. Little-boy Rich sat in that bar sipping Cherry Coke out of a highball glass, plucking out maraschino cherries with a tiny plastic musketeer sword. His father sat next to him, severely drunk. The Cubs played and lost on a black-and-white television. His father told him he'd grow up and into a fine ballplayer. His father told him he'd grow up and into a fine ballplayer several times there at the bar, because he'd forget what he'd said the moment he'd said it. Each time he said it, Rich simply smiled and said, "OK, Dad, I will."

Rich wondered if his father had known the Green Mill. Odds were good.

***

Rich and Francesca approached the front door hand in hand, soaked from the alley rain. The doorman held the door for them as they walked in together, giving Francesca a familiar nod, as if they knew each other. He looked at Rich with suspicion, but said nothing.

The Green Mill looked unlike the many other bars Rich had been in with his father. It was darker inside than outside in the night. The only real light came from behind the actual bar, where the bartenders required it to read the value of the bills they deposited into a hulking, old-fashioned steel cash register. People spoke in whispers so as not to overpower the blues trio playing softly on an old wooden stage. The patrons looked different, but not as different as the Lavender Line passengers. There were no elves, goblins, or house-cat conductors. Still, this was no ordinary bar. It was like an estuary between the city Rich already knew and the one he had discovered with Francesca.

Francesca ordered her usual concoction. The bartender acknowledged her with a wink and offered her a bar towel to dry off. Rich ordered a double Manhattan, for no reason other than he'd heard a man in an expensive-looking suit order it once. The man in the expensive-looking suit had looked and sounded a class above. Rich wanted nothing more than to appear a class above in this place, especially in the eyes of Francesca.

As Rich waited for his drink, he wondered what a double represented, and what a Manhattan might contain. "No possible way it could taste worse than Malört," he thought. A Manhattan sounded too fancy to be disgusting, but when the drink came, he found it quite disgusting, except for the maraschino cherry garnish, which made it tolerable. Rich felt saved by the cherry garnish, and requested more maraschino cherries from the bartender. As he did so, he noticed a decorative china plate behind the bar. A short poem was written on it. Rich read it aloud:

You've lost your job,
You've lost your dough,
Your jewels and handsome houses,
But things could be worse, you know,
You haven't lost your trousers

Francesca explained the poem. "It's a sick valentine from long ago, when this bar was a speakeasy. The Moran gang left the valentine in Jack McGurn's hand, after they shot him to pieces. Left a nickel in his other hand. Poor Jackie, he wasn't so bad. The boy he was reminds me of you."

Rich looked past Francesca as she talked. He was distracted by a man seated alone across the room, within a large booth nearer to the stage. The man's face was turned toward the musicians. There were several empty beer glasses in front of him. The man bore a strong resemblance to Rich's father, but in the darkness it was hard to say for sure. Rich thought he should get a closer look, but when he made a move to get up, Francesca grabbed hold of his arm. She didn't say anything. She just looked at him, wide-eyed and serious, as if to say he should not go where he was going to go, to that table with the man who looked like his father. Rich sat back down, still looking at the man.

The blues band ended their set with a version of B.B. King's "There Must Be a Better World Somewhere." Soon after the band finished, a girl walked up to the stage wearing a Venetian-style mermaid mask of glowing pearls, brass barnacles, and silver seaweed. She carried a glass of something dark in one hand and a crumpled piece of paper in the other. The bar went eerily silent as she arranged herself on a stool at the center of the stage, every face in the place looking toward her. She read line by line from her paper into the microphone. Her voice was shaky and young.

This is what she said.

My name was Lucy.

I was born with no legs as most Midwestern mermaids are, but that was about all we had in common. I had no fins or gills or dorsals. Couldn't hardly swim. Doctors called me "malformed," which is a doctor way of saying "deformed." My father explained the matter to me quite simply. He said I had no legs because I was a mermaid, and who wouldn't want to be a mermaid? I liked that explanation.

I was given the gift of legs at seven years old. A local shoe and table maker by the name of Simon Simantz manufactured for me two legs out of goatskin leather and birch. I did not take to them. I lurched awkwardly from foot to foot like a circus dog strutting on her hind legs. This of course gave my schoolmates a good laugh. They called me "Lucy leather legs" and sang mean songs about me.

Lucy leather
What's the weather
You shake like barley in the wind

One day in math class, I removed an ankle and smote the author of that awful song upon the skull with the force of God. The whole class laughed, and I was not disciplined, as a testament to the righteousness of my cause. When I returned home, father danced with me all around the parlor as if I were a mermaid princess. I will not forget that dance. It was my first and last with him or anyone.

I kept the legs on just long enough for my mother to drag me to a fancy studio in a fancy dress so that I might take one fancy picture as a whole human being for the sake of the family. I wonder if that picture survives me. It would be the only one. I am smiling in it only because the deceitful photographer tricked me into believing one of those puzzling Russian babushka doll props would be mine, should I obey his commands. I regretfully obeyed that trickster! In return for my smile, I got no more than a slap on the wrist from my mother for the trouble I gave.

The town we lived in was called Singapore, Michigan. You'll find that town now drowned under the waters of Lake Michigan. After the Great Chicago Fire, the town was completely deforested, supplying Chicago with lumber for rebuilding.

Without the trees, the winds and sands coming off the lake devoured the town. Within a few years, the place was no more than a poor man's Atlantis.

The town's demise secretly delighted me.

Soon after Singapore drowned, I found myself aboard a ferry headed for Chicago. The city when I first saw it was a curious misshapen illusion on the lake, like an amusement park funhouse full of those distorted mirrors. This phenomenon, I was told by our ship's captain, was known as a superior mirage, created by a rare concentration of warm over cold air. The fact saddened me. I had hoped for a moment the city was a malformity, like me.

In the city, I worked plucking chicken feathers within a giant stinking poultry factory from sunup to sundown six days a week, as was customary. The job was thankless and low paying. It was then I turned to the whiskey for relief. It was drunk by many of the factory workers with regularity, throughout the day. Soon I was named mermaid not because I swam in water, but because I swam in whiskey.

Until it became too expensive ...

Then I started on an opium tincture called laudanum. Laudanum was in fashion with the lower classes, cheaper than a bottle of liquor because it was not taxed as such, being still considered a medication.

The problem with laudanum was the frequent fainting spells, or overdoses, it caused.

Anyone who explains to you what an overdose feels like in any physical sense hasn't truly overdosed. If you could feel anything during an overdose, you wouldn't have overdosed, you'd have simply overdone. The real overdose is achieving the state of consciousness between earth and oblivion which conjurors seek; all characters of life, both living and dead, are with you, and there is no way to distinguish the real from the unreal. The body has no more feeling, and the brain no more consciousness, than that of a tree tilting in the wind. Then you wake up, or die.

My last overdose took place on the front door of the city, at Buckingham Fountain. I took a manly swig of an uncommonly powerful (and deadly) mixture of laudanum and gin. My head exploded with blinding fireworks as I tumbled backward, straight into the fountain. Under the waters, I saw other mermaids swimming about and riding on the backs of the great stone seahorse statues like sunken cowboys. One swam right up and kissed me on the lips! She tasted like rosewater. I held her hand as we swam out into Monroe Harbor, where we watched the moonrise bleach the city skyline.

The opiate overdose is a magnificent way to die.

When I was a girl, I visited my grandmother in this dreary mausoleum for the living called a "retirement home." As my father wheeled me down the deathly halls, the residents stared at me with wonder in their faded eyes. Most of the old residents were quiet, sad, and generally boring, at least in the eyes of a girl. I asked father why this was. He explained it was because most lively, entertaining people don't actually grow to be very old. He said the fun ones are much too adventurous to grow old, and so all tend to die young. He named this phenomenon the mermaid malady, after me, of course. He said I was doomed to a short life, the fun I was. He said there was never a mermaid lived to see a wrinkle in the mirror.

That is so.

The girl took her mask off and bowed to claps and whistles from the audience. Rich was fascinated with her story, and even more fascinated with the sight of her unmasked. She looked right at him, smiling with a smile so big, Rich figured it could've crushed all of Uptown. She was a beautiful Spanish girl with big brown eyes, khaki skin, and slithering black curls. She wore a fancy purple dress. She looked about Rich's age. Rich had never seen anything like her in the flesh, the simple reason being his neighborhood was not a Spanish neighborhood. Looking at her, he wished it was.

"What was that story?" Rich asked Francesca.

"Oh, that? That was just a Green Mill death rite. Here in this bar, it's a normal thing for an actor to dress up as a dead patron, then act a play, in summary of the dead patron's life. The dead patron in that case just happened to be a mermaid. When you die, someone will probably dress up in an expensive suit and look at a computer for an hour, and that will be a proper summary of the life of Richard the businessman!"

Rich nodded in confusion as he forced down his Manhattan a fraction of an ounce at a time. He started to feel dizzy. He must have looked it, too. The bartender stood in front of him and said, "A man has not drunk enough if he can still lie on the floor without holding on."

"Lucy was a mermaid, and our bartender was a comedian," Francesca explained. "There's a statue of Lucy's likeness on the lakeshore just south of Burnham Park, down on about 41st and Lake Shore Drive. She lies there on a piece of limestone as if taking a rest from a long swim, in full mermaid costume. Go there, you'll see it."[5]

Rich looked again at the table with the man who looked like his father. Rich wanted the man to be his father. His father had been a playful, kind man, and when he was sober there were happy days, but those had been mostly forgotten after his untimely death. Rich wondered if it would really be so strange to encounter the dead that night, when it seemed the impossible had become possible. Rich figured if his father's ghost was anywhere, it would be at a bar.

---

[5] *Francesca was right. Go there, and you will see it.*

Rich rose again to approach the man, when Francesca grabbed his arm. "We must be on our way to the Aragon Castle, darling! The ball has already begun." She led Rich out by the hand, into the night, where the rain had turned to snow, and was now falling in great white doughy gobs.

If Rich had looked back as he ran down the street with Francesca, he'd have gotten a good look at the face of the man he thought was his father. The man stood in the front window of the Green Mill, quietly drunk, staring sadly after Rich until long after he had disappeared within the thick curtains of white snow. Behind the man, the shadows of drinkers and dancers and drunks cured themselves at the bar. No one would leave the Green Mill, not anytime soon. The snow was falling too hard, and looked too beautiful from the inside.

The blues trio retook the stage and played on, deep into the night.

Dressing for the weather is impossible in Chicago

Stray Seasons of a Fox

Francesca led Rich through the dark streets in the falling snow to the entrance of what looked like an out-of-service elevated L platform. It wasn't a stop Rich had ever seen. He couldn't even tell what color the line was. He guessed it was the Red Line, given how far north they were, but there were no signs indicating the color or the name of the stop. He followed Francesca through the abandoned depot, then slowly up a broken escalator to the platform.

The platform was partly covered by a meager awning, which provided some shelter from the wildly blowing snow. The storm seemed to have strengthened in the short time it took them to walk upstairs. The wind was sweeping the snow east toward the lake, along the train tracks in such a way that it was as though the tracks were built solely as a passage for the snow. A handful of old, overhanging lamplights twisted and turned in the wind above them, shining out of the dark like fluorescent snow globes. Rich and Francesca took cover behind an old wooden storage box under one of the awnings.

They had been waiting only a few minutes when Rich

observed a bespectacled red fox, dressed in a red plaid suit and matching hat, emerge from the stairs on the opposite side of the tracks. He carried a white laundry bag over his shoulder. Once on the platform, the fox stood out in the falling snow, unhindered by the elements, like some fox legionnaire at attention, misplaced in time. Francesca, Rich, and the red fox were the only three waiting.

Rich watched the fox, waiting for him to move, wondering how long he would stand there completely exposed to the wind and snow. But the fox hardly budged, aside from removing a shiny gold pocket watch from the inside of his suit, looking at it, placing it back in his pocket, and staring down the tracks. The fox fixed a monocle over his glasses to help him see. He performed the same routine every minute or so.

Given how the night had gone, Rich was hardly surprised by the appearance of the debonair fox. Still, he was curious who the fox was, and where he was going. Was he waiting for the train to take him to his foxhole? What did foxes do on Friday nights? Did red foxes ride Red Lines? Rich emerged from behind the storage box to ask the fox these questions, and more.

"Hey, Mr. Fox, why don't you get out of the snow?" Rich yelled across the short distance of tracks.

The fox clearly hadn't noticed Rich or Francesca until just then. At the sound of Rich's yell, he leapt back on his hind legs in a defensive stance so quickly that his hat fell off and went tumbling down the tracks with the wind and snow, revealing two tall, pointy fox ears. After a few seconds, the fox regained his composure. He approached his edge of the tracks and responded in a voice that sounded like a tin whistle. "It is a terrifying fright to make your acquaintance this night. Why don't you introduce yourself, sir? You are an accomplice to the wind in the theft of my top hat!"

"Sorry, Mr. Fox, I didn't mean to scare you. I'm Rich. What's your name?"

"My name is Mr. Fox," Mr. Fox responded gruffly.

"Glad to meet you, Mr. Fox. Where are you off to tonight?"

"East Side, obviously. I am waiting for the oh-so-slow Red Line. It is horribly late tonight, and every night it seems these days. I have to get to the old king, out in the harbor lighthouse at the breakwater of the river, on the horizon of the lake. The old king is the reason for the seasons and this damnable weather!"

"What's that supposed to mean?"

"What on earth do you think it means? What explanation did you have for something as strange as falling snow in fall, not to mention here on the North Side? Look at this weather!" The Fox held his paws in the air.

"I guess it *is* strange weather we have here. A little early to be snowing, that's for sure." Rich realized how erratic the weather had been all night. It had started ordinary, but since then had snowed, rained, and snowed some more. The wind was also temperamental.

"Well, of course the snow has come early. It never does come on time, not anymore. You see, the old king partitioned the city into the four sides some time ago, when he was still old by young standards, and the city was young by old standards. The old king decreed each side of the city should have its own season, as was customary for kingdoms of the time. The East Side received summer because of the many beaches, the water, and, of course, the magic. The North Side was given autumn for the many trees in that part of the city, so that they might be magnificently colored all year. The old king flipped a coin to decide which of the remaining two sides would get spring, and the South Side won it. The South Side was wild even back then, and so got all the wilder, being quickly overrun with the springtime wildflowers. The West Side got winter because there was no place left for it, and it has been a bit of a self-fulfilling prophecy for the West Side ever since, to be honest—more of the cold and less of everything else out there, wherever 'there' is. I'm not certain where the North and South Sides stop and the West Side begins."

"What you're saying doesn't make any sense at all," Rich said. "Every side of the city gets all four seasons, every single year. I've seen them all, and I only live on one side."

"Well, sure, nowadays you get all sorts of seasons on every side of the city throughout the year, but it wasn't always that way. The old king was old even in olden times, and he kept getting older and older, then even older than that. He's so old now, he's lost his wits entirely. He confuses seasons with seasonings, thinks the monarch is just a butterfly, and mistakes city sides for hors d'oeuvres. Just yesterday, the old king stood up in the middle of the night and took a piss on his pillow. I'm only returning from the cleaner just now." Mr. Fox held up his white laundry bag as proof of the bedwetting. "And there you have an explanation for this snowstorm in the heart of autumn. Half the time the old king doesn't know winter from summer, so seasons in the city stray like cats, just as they stray in his thoughts. If I wasn't around to set his gears straight, we'd have January in July and no use for a weather forecast at all!"

Francesca emerged as Mr. Fox finished. "Mr. Fox, will you tell the old king to awake the sleeping summer to sunshine and starlight, just for tonight? I would *so* like to see the stars at the ball. And I know Rich would as well. This cold snow will not do at all."

"For Francesca Finnegan, he may permit the perfection a midsummer's night. But why are you waiting for a train, if you are only off to the ball? The Aragon is just a walk down the block, after all. Simply head downstairs and—"

A faint train whistle interrupted Mr. Fox. A tiny, devilish will-o'-the-wisp formed down the tracks a short distance west. The light moved steadily closer, emerging in the form of a regular old Red Line plowing recklessly through the mounds of snow that had formed on the tracks. The train thundered into the station, causing a brief, blinding eruption of snow in all directions. Rich staggered back from the onslaught, covering his face with his arms. When he wiped the snow from his face, he looked toward the train to see where Mr. Fox was boarding. Through the windows, the train looked empty, something abnormal for any Red Line, at any time of night. The conductor car even looked empty. Rich couldn't make out where Mr. Fox had boarded, or if he was on the train, and in seconds, the train was disappearing around a bend in the tracks to the east.

"Mr. Fox will only ride the Red Line. Red Line for a red fox." Francesca looked over the railing onto the street below. "How silly of me! Mr. Fox was right. We are just a hop-skip away from the Aragon. It's been forever and a day since I was there. Come along, Rich, it's just down the street. We're late!"

The two headed back down the way they had come, onto the snow-covered street, where they walked only a block before turning onto an unusually quiet street with no signs, lights, cars, or people. The street narrowed as they moved down it and eventually became an alley. The street-turned-alley soon dead-ended into an unspectacular concrete wall with a single green door in the center. It wasn't what Rich had expected of a castle entrance, but in that way, it was no different from anything else he'd encountered that night. He'd come to expect the unexpected, and to like it.

A sign stood before the green door on a wooden tripod.

Welcome to the back door of the Aragon Castle

Private Ball hosted by Queen Billy Boyle of the last Chicago farm and her multitalented court, featuring the peculiar Polish Potawatomi. Music and dancing from 9 p.m. to 7 a.m., interrupted by a war dance at I forget when. Businessmen, bankers, and black suits strictly prohibited.

Rich followed Francesca past the sign, toward the door.

Just before they walked in, he noticed an abrupt change in the weather. The snow stopped, and the sky cleared of the storm. The stars shone down, suddenly bright, as if someone had flipped a switch and turned them on. A familiar, pleasantly warm wind blew in Rich's face and helped him recognize the season.

It was summer, in autumn.

The young are getting old and the summer is cold,
all the birds have been singing at night

Glow-in-the-Dark Stars

Castles come in all shapes and sizes. Some are made for war and have arrow slits for windows carved within thick stone walls. Some are made for revelry, surrounded with hills of barley for malting and drinking within great dining halls. Some castles are barren, suffocated throughout with wild ivy and the roaming ghosts of dead kings and queens. Mythical castles sit on clouds in the sky, and are accessible only through stories like this, by those who still believe stories like this.

On the night Rich visited it, the Aragon was something like one of those mythical castles, but only on that night. Today, it's just an ordinary Aragon.

***

Rich strolled through the back door of the Aragon as coolly as he could manage. He was as nervous as ever, because he'd never been to a ball, or on an official date with a girl. What would Francesca expect him to do? Dance, drink? *Kiss*? He had no idea how to kiss, but if it came to that, he was determined to do it as coolly as possible. He repeated the words "be cool" over and over in his head, like a lunatic.

Whatever coolness Rich had mustered melted away the instant he saw the inside of the Aragon. The whole hall was painted with the dazzling brush of thousands of candles burning in straight orange arrows toward the sky. There was fire everywhere. It was a pyromaniac fantasy: candles dangled from chandeliers, stood on tables, and danced in midair. The candlelight created marvelous, ever-changing colors and shadows. It seemed to Rich there were no light bulbs anywhere, and what was more, there was no ceiling anywhere. The candles reached up into an unobstructed, starry night. Tassels of stardust flowed in and around masses of beaming stars, and it seemed to Rich that every single nerve, vein, and artery of the universe was revealed to him in a glance toward the sky.

Then there was the ballroom, which didn't much look like a ballroom. It looked more like a medieval village faire at night, with the strangest sort of villagers. The ballroom's focal point was a royal court, situated on a slightly elevated stone platform at the far center of the hall. On the platform, a little girl in a faded white summer dress sat upon a comically oversized throne. She had a smile on her face and dangled her feet playfully. Rich recognized her as the girl he had seen drifting through the sky earlier in the night, described to him by Doctor Denlinger of Dunning on the Lavender Line as the queen of the last city farm. The queen's hands were bound to the chair with leather straps, so that she might not be swept away by an errant wind. Next to the queen's throne stood the grand duke, as if he were highest in her service. He was easily recognizable from a distance, with his massive mustache and corncob pipe. A girl piper, wearing a crown of gleaming red-leaf skeletons, played her pipes for the queen and danced a childish dance around the huge throne. Below the queen, at the base of the stairs leading up to the throne, two fauns armed with long pikes stood at attention.

Behind the royal court, a magnificent tapestry bearing a coat of arms hung from the wall. Rich recognized its design from the label on the Malört he'd regrettably tasted earlier in the night. The design had the same silhouette of a man's face upon a white shield, his mouth bound shut with the city flag. On the adjacent wall hung an equally magnificent tapestry of similar design with a few subtle yet distinct differences. For one, the silhouette's mouth was not bound shut. Instead, the man's mouth was open, and the small figure of a fairy flew out of it. Various other fantasy creatures could be seen in the background of the tapestry, all around the man's face.

The queen's court overlooked a busy ball floor surrounded by several pillars, which held up a circular second-story balcony. Behind the pillars were two- and three-story cottages designed in the Moorish architectural style, like something out of *Arabian Nights*. These cottages contained roaring house parties, dense with ball-goers. Most also had balconies outside their onion domes, overflowing with guests. From below, the balconies resembled the mysterious platforms overlooking the streets of the French Quarter during Mardi Gras, inaccessible to the curious onlooker, filled with the masked faces of glamorously disguised Cajuns observing the streets below.

The ball was an assembly of all the odd and amazing creatures from the adventures of the night. Rich was startled at the sight of a giant obelisk of a man, wearing what at first glance looked like a terrifying mask of some forest monster, complete with buck horns and a moss-covered face. Rich wondered if it was truly a mask, or if it was the Riverview machinist himself. Next, he saw Doctor Denlinger of Dunning across the hall, brandy balloon in hand, cigar in mouth, admiring the tapestry featuring his city flag. A fine wind blew through the hall, hardly noticeable yet very much present, as if it were itself a guest. Rich was surprised to see Templeton conscious and fully functioning at the bar, drinking with vigor out of a thimble-sized glass. Rich decided to walk over and say hello.

As Rich approached the bar, he passed the original feline Lavender Line conductor, who, in his discussions with a legless girl in a wheelchair, remarked, "Should a mermaid die of alcoholic liver disease, it will state on the death certificate that the mermaid died of natural causes." The girl nodded her head in agreement, then drank a long drink from a steel flask.

At the bar, Templeton greeted Rich enthusiastically. "Goshamighty! Rich the elf savior! Rich the hero! Welcome to the hero club. I know you will love it as much as I love it. Let me tell you, being a hero is an EXCELLENT business. Thank you for leaving the conductor that note on the train window. He woke me up at the right stop, and also made sure I hadn't died. Have a try of this amber ale and give us your first reaction to the flavor of it."

Templeton handed Rich a miniature glass of beer. Rich drank it and declared all he could. "Tastes all right, a little bitter."

"Hops, sir! Hops! You're mad as hops. You and the old fairy king! But you must be mad as hops before you can be sober as raindrops. So have another taste!" Templeton laughed crazily.

"Where's the king?" Rich asked. It was a just question. There was a queen in attendance, but no king at her side. Templeton sang a strange poem in response.

> High on the harbor
>   The old king sits
> He's now so old and gray
>   He's nigh lost his wits
> With a bridge of white mist
>   Irving Park he crosses
> On his stately journeys
>   From Pilsen to Rosehill's crosses
> Or going up with music
>   On blowing snowy nights
> To sup with the queen
>   Of the cold starry lights

The bartender poured Templeton another tiny glass out of a little wood barrel, about the size of a large pop can, positioned on the bar. Templeton poured it down his throat in an instant, then stood upon the bar and made the following proclamation, a wild look of delight in his eyes.

Look: More golden than that milk from the tits of a royal consort, whose tits I once consorted.

Smell: Hints of pine, thyme, and lost time.

Taste: If intemperance had a taste, it would taste of this. The only thing I've tasted better was a Tuscan princess called Maria de' Medici, who is now buried in a sand dune at Montrose Beach.

Feel: How strange it is to be thirsty, have a drink of something to quench that thirst, then to be even thirstier than before. I am parched almost to death after one sip!

Overall: In the words of someone romantic, "The course of true love never did run smoother."

Templeton tried to curtsy, but shuddered on the way down and lost his footing. He tumbled backward behind the bar, to laughs and claps from the small circle of onlookers.

Rich laughed so hard, he hardly felt the graze on his butt cheek. A second later, he felt the graze again, followed by a hard pinch like a bee sting on the same cheek. Turning around, he was surprised to find before him the girl piper he'd seen dancing circles around the throne of the queen. He recognized her from the crown of bright red-leaf skeletons on her head.

"Hi there?" Rich asked, like the boy gentleman he was. He looked down on her smiling. She was about three feet high and stared up at him with fierce, revelator eyes, a look deserving a face much bigger and scarier than the one she had.

"Hi there yourself," the little piper responded, in a tone of contempt. "What *are* you doing here?" She asked the question as if she already knew him, and knew he didn't belong.

"I'm doing here with Francesca Finnegan. What are *you* doing here?" Rich realized Francesca was not at his side.

"What am I doing here! What am *I* doing here!" The girl was almost screaming, her face a red apple. "Have you ever heard of the piper at the gates of dawn? HAVE YOU?"

"No."

She circled Rich like a little lioness. "The piper at the gates of dawn is the wind in the willows, and I am the breeze through Bronzeville! Did you not think there was a piper at the gates of night? Did you not know all cities except one grow up? Where did you think you *were*? Who do you think you *are*?"

"I guess … I guess I never really thought about it." Rich babbled nervously, looking around for Francesca. He had no idea what the little girl was talking about, or what she wanted with him.

"I'll see to it you'll not ever remember me, not this night, not yourself in it!" The girl put her pipes in her mouth and skipped away, for the time being.

Rich turned from the bar, too confused at the encounter

to consider what the piper girl's threat had meant, or who she might be.

Where had Francesca gone?

He hadn't seen her since the two had walked in. He peered through the crowded ballroom, up to the stage where the girl queen sat bound to her throne, then back across the ball floor, to the entrance, and up into the sparkling sky above. There he found her, almost as he'd once again forgotten her. He saw her up within the window of a globe-shaped, third-story keep, nestled above one of the many cottages lining the exterior of the hall. She stood staring down at him, still as a statue, and might have been mistaken for one, were it not for her unmistakable blue hair. She looked at him as if she were waiting for him, as if she expected him to come to her.

So he did.

Rich made his way through the crowd to the cottage, then through another more crowded crowd within the cottage to a narrow spiral staircase. The staircase took him up through the second floor, which was also quite crowded. He received not a few curious glances from the crowd as he quickly made his way up to the third floor, and Francesca.

The third floor was a round, plain, dimly lit room with nothing in it but a single twin bed, a large standing mirror, and a candle upon a small dresser. Francesca was nowhere to be found. Rich made his way to the window, where he looked down onto the crowded floor of the Aragon, searching for her. He was distraught at her not being there, but only for the minute she wasn't there. As he looked for her out the window, she surprised him from behind, with either a whisper or a song—in that moment, he wasn't sure if it was her regular voice that made a sound like music, or if she was actually singing to him. As he listened to her, the clatter from the Aragon below died away like sounds already in the past.

She did finally kiss him then, up in the little round room, above the crowd below, within the window for all to see. It was Rich's first real kiss, and when it happened, it seemed to him the room spun round and round with gravity-defying speed, as if they were riding an out-of-control merry-go-round. They spun and spun, going so fast, they eventually found themselves pinned together against the wall, paralyzed by the centrifugal force of the spinning room. Neither minded it. For Rich, it was the ecstasy of a carnival ride. Perhaps he would never know who Francesca was, from where she came, or where she was going, but he saw her in that moment, apart from the mystery, and she was simply a girl.

But the spinning of the room stopped as quickly as it had started, causing Rich and Francesca to break apart with a startle. They were interrupted by an unexpected, gale-force wind, which had burst through the hall out of nowhere, instantly quenching every one of the candles lighting the party. Francesca and Rich peered down into the blackness of the ball, where a disorderly crowd of muttering, confused guests added to their own sense of confusion.

The wind stopped, and the entire hall was relit by the poof of a tall, roaring bonfire, which sprung up as if by magic in the center of the dance floor. Claps and cheers came from the crowd, as if this were all a planned segment of the night's entertainment. The crowd quieted, all eyes on the flames sending sparks like offerings into the night sky. Rich and Francesca stood hand in hand, waiting for whatever show this could be, if it was a show at all.

Looking down into the crowd, Rich saw a narrow path clear for what appeared to be an Indian, making his way toward the fire. Rich hadn't seen the Indian anywhere in the ball until then. He crept up to the fire alone, stoking it with a long peace pipe. The Indian, aside from his dress, didn't look the part. He was tall, with bushy blond hair and fair skin that shone through a drenching of multicolored war paint. Rich guessed correctly who the new guest was: the notorious Polish Potawatomi, described to him by Kinzie during their walk through the woods.

The audience around the fire crowded closer, mesmerized as the Indian circled the flames, scanning the room cautiously for someone or something. Rich shivered as the Indian's eyes passed over him. The Potawatomi took an enormous drag of his peace pipe, his eyes continuing to search the room. Then a look of surprise came over his face, as if he'd just woken from a dream, or was a newly arrived guest in someone else's. He put his pipe down and began a slow dance around the fire, chanting a deep series of ancient war songs low under his breath.

As the Indian danced, familiar night shadows were cast about the room in all directions, to the fascination of Rich and the rest of the crowd. The girl piper's pipes shrieked at the dark, approaching form of the Lavender Line, circling the trim of the upper walls. Oohs and aahs echoed. The queen and her court turned in amazement at the shape of a Ferris wheel spinning on the wall behind them, upon the tapestry. The silhouette of a Malört bottle shone darkly upon the bar, where the crowd laughed in unison at the sight of Templeton twirling a drunken war dance of his own. The smoke from the fire formed the shape of a mermaid above the tips of the flames, rising higher in the air, where it swam about to claps and gasps from the crowd.

As Rich watched, he wondered if this was one of those last war dances Kinzie had referred to in his description of the Potawatomi. He sensed it was that, yet also something else. The dance was like a solemn, beautiful funeral ceremony encapsulating all the childish associations and memories he had encountered within the course of this strange night. Nothing was omitted.

The Polish Potawatomi danced faster and faster, as his war chant rose to a crescendo. A disturbing black mural of a farm blowing away in the wind could be seen for a few seconds on each of the walls. On the dance floor, the map from the grand duke's residence near Rhine Falls appeared in all its many colors. The shadows of a little boy and girl could be seen chasing each other throughout the hall, up the stairs onto a balcony and down through the dance floor, meandering among the revelers, who gasped in wonder, then clapped in humor. In the instant before the boy shadow caught the girl, the Polish Potawatomi's chant reached its peak.

Then, several things happened at once.

The wind returned with renewed strength, whipping through the hall with a force that lifted the little queen from her seat as easily as if she were a feather, sending her spiraling wildly into the night sky with a squeak of a scream Rich hardly heard above the howling of the wind. The grand duke made a clumsy lunge for her but was blown clear off the back of the stage himself, along with the two fauns who had guarded the queen. The last Rich saw of the queen was a white dot, almost indistinguishable from the stars, flying through the sky like a comet.

During the queen's unintended departure, the massive bonfire was extinguished as easily as a lone birthday candle. The hall was cast into darkness. The Polish Potawatomi stopped his singing, and for a second, all that could be heard was the sound of the wind and the drowned-out cries from the panic-stricken crowd. Those cries turned to screams of horror when the sound of gunfire rang out. Rich found the source of the gunfire near the entrance to the ballroom, where he recognized the figure of Kinzie under a ray of moonlight, charging his way through the crowd in a straight line toward the Polish Potawatomi, who stood now with his tomahawk at his side. Kinzie and the Polish Potawatomi met violently near the ashes of the bonfire, and the crowd fled from them in a frenzy.

It seemed to Rich the ball was over.

But from the time he'd first kissed Francesca to the point when he'd realized the ball was over, he'd been entirely distracted, almost separated from his own senses, by the chaos unfolding below him. He hadn't noticed Francesca leave the round room, but when he turned from the window, he found she was gone. Looking back down into the ball, searching for her within the pandemonium, he found her dancing in circles like a crazy person, together with the little piper girl. Rich rushed down the spiral staircase, hopeful he might leave with her.

When he ran into the chaos of the ball, he saw Francesca again, walking away alone, toward the back door where they'd entered. He yelled for her but could hardly hear his own voice through the wind, still wailing a deafening blow. He raised his arms to motion for her, but found the air had suddenly become a blizzard of blowing confetti. The confetti swarmed his arms, hiding them, so he ran toward her. Finally, she noticed him. And then she ran away.

She fled with a smile on her face, looking back over her shoulder, as if this were just a game, not unlike the one they'd played when they had first met. Rich would of course play, confident he was the faster and could catch her as he'd caught her once before. He raced after her through the clutter of the ballroom, over the ashes of the fire between the Polish Potawatomi and Kinzie, then in and out of several cottages, upstairs, out windows, over the queen's empty throne, behind the bar where Templeton lay unconscious, back to where the chase had started, and over again.

And then again.

He chased her and chased her, but it seemed to Rich there was no catching her, not this time. Francesca was the faster of the two, but no faster than she had been earlier in the night. Rich was just slower.

The end of it happened like this: Rich continued to trail her with a stubborn (and slow) persistence, finally reaching a wide stone staircase near the front entrance of the hall, which Francesca danced up with mocking ease, as if she were flying. Rich himself made it only halfway up the stairs. By that point, he was so out of breath he felt suffocated. His lungs were crowded by his giant pounding heart, which rattled the bones in his chest. He collapsed onto his hands and knees, then rolled with great effort onto his back, where he lay in a daze, strewn across the stairs, thoroughly defeated.

The last thing Rich saw was the ceiling. How peculiar, you might think, because all throughout the ball, there had been no ceiling. That is true. And the ceiling Rich saw didn't look much different from no ceiling at all. The ceiling looked painted with glow-in-the-dark stars, as if the real stars had been frozen in time, a picture of exactly where they were in the sky that night. Go to the Aragon today and you'll see the painted stars exactly as they looked the night of the ball. They remain there, frozen in a spell of surprise from the madness below them.

The last thing Rich heard was the whistle from the little piper girl's pipes, like a bewitchment. It was a lullaby, a slower version of some song he'd heard before, maybe when he was a little boy, too young to remember or recognize anything other than a melody. Rich closed his eyes and, concentrating on remembering, forgot.

He forgot everything.

He forgot the Lavender Line, Riverview, Templeton,

Malört, the grand duke, and the Green Mill. He forgot Francesca last of all, just before he lost consciousness, as the confetti tickled his face and the piper girl's pipes played on. His memory of all that had happened in the night would not return until years later, when he awoke from a tumble on a downtown city sidewalk, as an adult, as Richard K. Lyons, vice president of something.

III

"I sang a stout, a draught, a bout of gout.
A dream is no dream without her about."

Transfiguration

The Brown Line to Andy

Remember, our Richard the rich had just bumped his head when we left him.

This was all-grown-up Richard, a fine specimen of a businessman, on his way to happy hour after he'd closed the great Goldman Sachs deal of deals. He'd bumped his head, *hard*, right after casting his golden pen into the river like a champion gold-pen javelinist. His knees had buckled beneath his fat stomach, after the ill-fated crow hop, and he'd gone down hard, nearly knocking himself out cold on a sewer cap. He had lain in front of the little homeless fairy-tale salesgirl, in the middle of a Michigan Avenue sidewalk, bleeding out of his ear.

Then, the little girl played a song for Richard—a song he'd heard before.

As Richard lay there half-conscious, admiring the darkening sky, he remembered all that had happened on the night with Francesca. The song the fairy-tale salesgirl played was a song he knew from that night. The salesgirl played it on her little wooden pan flute, and it was like a spell. Francesca, Templeton, the Lavender Line, the Aragon, the

Polish Potawatomi, and every other odd remembrance came rushing back.

After lying there awhile, Richard was shaken to his senses and helped up by some passing stranger. When he rose to his feet and steadied himself, he saw a view of the city he'd not seen since he was a boy. And how spectacular the view was! You'd have to remember how incredible the city appeared the first time you laid eyes on it to comprehend what it looked and felt like to Richard in that moment, but even if you could remember, you wouldn't be able to relive it as Richard was. The city seemed a kingdom, with shiny towers of silver and gold. It boomed in mechanical and electrical notes. Cars, trains, planes, and people bustled below, above, all around him. The city felt like something made of magic.

The city felt brand new.

Richard stood dumbstruck as people filed past him in faceless waves. He studied the faceless faces as they passed. They were all unrecognizable, except for one. In that one face, he saw something of himself, and where the city was silver and gold, what he saw was drab and gray, because he saw himself in that moment as he now saw the city— through the eyes and mind of the boy he once was. After he saw himself, he was sad at all he'd become. He'd become everything Francesca predicted and worse. He was the simple, surly vice president of something.

Richard wondered how he'd become what he'd become, and how he could have forgotten Francesca and all that had happened that night. The memories had been dormant for years, and those years had passed by as quickly as the city people were passing him on the street. Why had he only now remembered the adventure he'd forgotten, within the city he'd forgotten?

His mind wandered back through the events of the night with Francesca, in search of an answer. He wandered through the game of ghost in the graveyard to the Lavender Line, through Riverview and Rhine Falls, all the way to the Green Mill, then finally to the Aragon. After he'd lost consciousness on the stairs of the Aragon, he remembered waking up in the middle of a park, in the middle of the city, feeling all Rip Van Winklish. The little piper girl's song had been replaced with police sirens. The tickle on his face wasn't confetti at all. It was a drifting of autumn leaves passing over his face. The stars in the sky were mostly disappeared, hiding behind a purple veil of clouds. He looked around, recognizing the park he was in, the same park where earlier in the night he'd played ghost in the graveyard. He lay in the very spot where he'd once caught Francesca, though when he'd caught her then, the field had been filled with players and spectators. When he awoke, it was empty. He remembered how confused he'd been. He asked himself what had happened in the time between the moment he'd caught the mysterious girl and the moment he'd awakened.

What had caused him to forget it all?

He found his answer inside the Aragon. He remembered the girl piper playing her music as he lay on the stairs, at the end of the night, and it dawned on him why he'd recognized the homeless fairy-tale salesgirl and her song. She was the same "piper at the gates of night" from the ball. Her appearance was unchanged. Her song was the same. He remembered how she'd played the memory of the night away, after he'd lost Francesca. Had she just played it all back for him?

Richard looked to where the girl had been begging on the sidewalk, but she wasn't there. She was nowhere. The only trace of her was a crown of red-leaf skeletons, and the sign she had camped next to, which still read:

Caution, Falling MIce

Richard stepped cautiously back from the sign, looking up. He preferred not to be crushed by falling ice. And he preferred not to consider the days gone by, the early mornings sacrificed to become the vice president of something, washed away in the late nights of boozy, blacked-out oblivion.

He wondered what it would be like to be the vice president of nothing. The thought brought a smile to his face. Just as it did, his phone buzzed with a familiar series of text messages:

Wherefore art thou, King Richard?

The white queen is frisky

From the red whisky :)

Richard wouldn't respond to the text. He wouldn't go to the bar. He had no interest in the red whiskey or the white queen. His heart was changed. He'd go home, in hopes of catching his son, Andy, before bed. He'd tell Andy a bedtime story. He had a new story to tell, after all.

He'd just remembered it.

***

Richard made for the Brown Line to home and Andy. The platform he caught the train on was dense with commuters sweating buckets under heavy winter coats and hats. The weather had warmed considerably since the cold morning, as though the winter had forgotten it was winter. Richard thought of Mr. Fox, and of how he wouldn't be the least bit surprised at the abrupt change in temperature.

Richard bobbed and weaved his way through the thick crowd toward the track, where he strategically positioned himself to squeeze onto the next train, which he knew would be overcrowded to the point he might not be able to fit in. But he had to fit. He was determined not to be late. As the Brown Line chugged pathetically around a bend in the distance, the crowd tensed, preparing to storm the train for passage, the thought of waiting the additional three to five minutes for the next train unthinkable. The train cars maxed out the instant the doors opened. Richard pushed his way in desperately. He was one of the last to squeeze aboard, wedged tightly between the doors and the weight of the rest of the bloated car.

As the train inched along, Richard thought of the Lavender Line, of how different it was in every way from the Brown. Yes, both were technically trains, but that was all they had in common. No one wanted to be on the Brown

Line. The Brown Line was barely operable. That particular Brown Line had broken, blinking lights, stank of shit, stalled frequently, and couldn't exceed twenty miles per hour due to the dangerously full passenger load. And the passenger load was a collection of the most miserable marketeers, accountants, bricklayers, consultants, and other sad souls Richard could ever remember seeing. What he'd give for a seat on the Lavender Line. Just a seat with the wind blowing through him, as he dreamed of the wind blowing through him.

The ride was slow, as usual, so to pass the time, Richard surfed through the far reaches of the Internet on his phone. He searched for Templeton Goodfellow, Francesca Finnegan, and the Lavender Line, finding no direct evidence of their existence, only some clues. He learned there had once been a cable-car system running under the city, before the L was introduced, as Francesca had described it. The cable-car system had, according to the Internet, been out of operation for one hundred years. He learned there had once been an insane asylum called Dunning, also closed for about one hundred years. He learned there had once been a vast amusement park on Chicago's North Side, called Riverview, which had been closed for about fifty years.

During more of his searches—on the Great Chicago Fire, George Gipp, John Kinzie, Fort Dearborn—Richard somehow stumbled on his own LinkedIn profile. He read through his vice-president-of-something résumé and the rest of the prestigious positions in business he'd held over the course of his career. He was surprised to find he didn't care for his professional history, which looked now like a list of meaningless tasks he'd rather not do again. LinkedIn itself looked like a cemetery of childhood dreams, strangely published within an online directory. Richard changed his profile title to "Vice President of Fishery and Nunchuckery, skilled in the art of the roundhouse kick," and felt much better for having done so. He looked up from his phone and smiled. The train was emptying. He had room to breathe.

He was almost home.

Richard's was the last stop on the line, his house a half-mile north of the depot. When the train finally reached his stop, he burst through the doors, taking off as fast as he could up the street toward home. He had no time to lose. His son would soon be fast asleep. It was already nearly as dark as the city would get, the sky its usual not-so-dark purple, dotted with airplane lights where the stars once shone.

Richard stumbled through the front door of his house a heaping, huffing, disgusting mass of sweat. He staggered through a short hallway and into the living room, where he collapsed on the soft carpet. As he lay there, he saw his wife and son lying together only a few feet from him on the couch, under a blanket, staring at him, frozen with surprise. *The Lego Movie* played on the television, the song "Everything Is Awesome" blaring.

His son leapt down from the couch and smiled a long, slow smile, then ran toward him. When the boy reached Richard, he looked down at him, touched his face, and clapped his hands.

"Where *were* you, Daddy?"

Richard was finally home. Time for bed. Time for a story.

He carried Andy up the stairs to his room. He wrestled the boy into his pajamas, then wrestled the boy some more. After the wrestling, they jumped on the bed until Richard's wife scolded them from downstairs. They sang songs and howled at the winter moon together like wolves. After another scolding, and a not at all quiet game of hide and seek (and another scolding), they settled down together onto a rocking chair in a corner of the room, near a window overlooking the backyard. It had started to snow. There on the chair, the last and most important of bedtime rituals began: the story that must be told before the boy could fall asleep.

Richard told Andy one of those once-upon-a-time fairy tales, in which a boy and a girl set out on a series of unbelievable adventures in some imaginary world, with inhabitants of the most unimaginable sort. The boy sat spellbound as he listened to his father tell the story with an uncharacteristic enthusiasm. The boy and the girl traveled through secret amusement parks, valleys, woods, under waterfalls, aboard hidden underground trains, all the way to a castle, for an extravagant ball. Along the way, they encountered flying queens, grand dukes, talking foxes, cowboys and Indians, mermaids, sprites, elves, and more. At the end of it all, the girl gave the boy a kiss. The kiss made the boy's head spin and spin, and as it spun, the boy lost the girl. He looked around for her, even chased after her, but the girl wasn't meant to be found or caught. The girl was one of those fairies you hear about only in fairy tales—the kind that can't be found by the likes of you or me. Those fairies are content to simply roam the hidden fairy kingdoms, occasionally inviting one of us in to play, and sometimes more. Sometimes they meddle in our affairs, just for the fun of it. All fairies do is play, after all. And when they've finished playing, everyone lives happily ever after.

Richard looked down at Andy. The boy was asleep, dreaming dreams of fairy adventures.

Richard looked out the window. The light snowfall had turned into a blizzard. He lifted Andy's limp body from the rocking chair, lay his son down gently in his bed, kissed him on the forehead, then proceeded downstairs to learn what his wife did for fun on Friday nights.

His wife was wandering about the kitchen, nervously cleaning, sipping from a wine glass. Richard asked what she did for fun on Friday nights. She said she didn't know what she did for fun on Friday nights. She said she usually just waited for him on Friday nights. Now that he was home, she didn't know what to do. Richard suggested they play a game. She said she would like nothing more than to play a game.

So they played a game until late into the night. It was the first real game Richard had played since ghost in the graveyard. And he loved it.

***

After that fateful winter day, Richard passed from the dark age of his life. He retired from his vice presidency of something in favor of some other work, work he actually enjoyed. The end of his vice presidency of something depressurized him, body and soul. The years of his life faded from him, and he remembered what it was to be a boy again.

"Call me Rich," he'd say with a wink.

He lost his ability as a businessman and instead became skilled in the art of hiding and seeking, London Bridging, Red Rovering, and all those other things businessmen can't do. He made chubby snow angels. He rolled down hills for the dizziness. He ate candy for dinner. He played games. He played and played.

For Rich, the games stalled the passage of time. The world spun less swiftly and madly than it had before, when he'd wanted it to spin that way. The new time gave him extra time to look to the sky, as he had promised himself he would do on the Ferris wheel at Riverview, with Francesca. He looked up and off into the distance, mostly at sunset, with his son, and when the moon rose, the two threw rocks at it, trying to hit it, for fun. One night, his son hit the moon square in the forehead with a powerful shot, knocking it out of the sky. The moon came splashing down into Lake Michigan and took a whole day to rise from the water again, far out on the horizon, in the place where the city ends and the rest of the world begins.

***

The years passed slowly, but they passed all the same. Rich noticed they'd passed when, one day, he found himself suddenly standing face to face with Andy. Rich couldn't believe it. The boy was turning into a man. Andy had reached the point when a boy can outlast his parents into the night, an important milestone in the lives of all concerned. It was a Friday when he outlasted them for the first time, sometime late in autumn. It was one of those nights when the neighborhood kids converge on the parks for games.

After dinner, Andy set forth to play a game of kick the can, jailbreak, or ghost in the graveyard. From an upstairs bedroom, Rich looked down on his son running off through the blowing leaves. It was as windy as ever, one of those autumn nights when the winds suddenly rise, separating all the dying leaves from the trees, scattering them on the ground in globs of red and yellow. The trees swayed loudly, but Rich liked the sound of the loud sway. It made him sleepy. He lay down in bed with the sleeping music of swinging trees in his ears and the shadows of leaves twirling overhead. He closed his eyes and imagined Andy playing games. He imagined Andy running circles in a field under barren trees come to life like dancing skeletons in the wind. The sky darkened from pink to purple, relinquishing daylight as the orange streetlights took control. It was then, as night set in, when the game took an unusual turn. Andy didn't see from where she came, but she was there, standing casually in the middle of the park. She was a girl unlike the other girls. She had a reputation for never having been caught, but she looked worth catching. Her eyes were not the color of eyes, and her hair was not the color of hair. She looked at him, inviting him to chase her, inviting him to play with her.

And he would …

And they all lived happily ever after…

A Flight of Spirits

Years later, after Rich had become old and gray, after his son, Andy, was a man with children of his own, after *nearly* everything, he took a walk. He walked up the coast of Lake Michigan, somewhere on the northern edge of the city. Old man Rich liked to walk. He'd take long walks around sunset, when the temperature was cooler and the sun lower. Toward the evenings, his feet felt less heavy beneath him, his back less bent behind him.

Old man Rich hadn't been walking for long when he felt a storm blowing down with the wind from over the lake. He was surprised. He hadn't expected it to storm. His old eyes squinted at the forecast on his phone. It said no chance of rain, but he knew it was coming. He understood the unpredictable nature of weather in the city, and he could smell the rain in the distance, out over the lake, headed straight for him. He thought he'd better head home, before the storm arrived.

He made his way from the lakefront into the city. He decided to catch his old friend the L home. These days he rode the L for fun. A ride felt like a guided tour through the history of his life. He liked to sit and look out the windows at the scenes of his past, as they passed. It helped him remember, if only for a little while. In his old age, he couldn't always remember, not even for a little while.

By the time Rich reached the L, the storm was at hand. His old chicken legs strained up the steps and onto the platform. Strangely, there was no one waiting for the train on either side. The station looked abandoned, or out of service. Rich looked down the tracks for any sign of an approaching train. Nothing.

Something was wrong.

Rich paced back and forth along the platform for a few minutes, worried about the rain, wondering about the train. He hoped the train would come soon, but it didn't, and there was no one to ask why, or where it was. After another few minutes, with the sky overhead diabolical, Rich decided that the train wasn't coming, and that he should find some other way home.

Just as he was turning to leave, something red flashed from within the stairwell on the opposite platform. When he looked in the direction of the red, he saw a fluffy tail disappearing down the stairs. He thought of a Mr. Fox he'd once met on an empty train platform, much like the one he was on, what seemed like a lifetime before. Had he just seen the same Mr. Fox? Rich guessed it was probably his old eyes playing tricks on him, but there was only one way to be sure. He walked back down the L stairs, out into the street.

The downpour began just as Rich reached the street. It was raining so hard on the hot pavement, a misty evaporation rose off the ground into the air. In the haze, Rich spotted the red outline of a small, unmistakably furry figure hurrying away down the sidewalk, holding a newspaper over his head to protect him from the rain.

Definitely a fox.

Rich ran after the fox as fast as his old, wobbly legs would carry him. He was soaked, but he liked the feel of the rain. It cooled him as he ran, and he felt like he was running as fast as he'd ever run. He laughed and splashed through puddles. The rain washed in and out of his mouth and tasted sweet as soda, like it had once before, and when he swallowed it, he felt as though he might live forever. He hadn't felt that way since the night he'd splashed through an alley with Francesca.

Rich chased Mr. Fox a few blocks west, until he'd nearly caught him at the corner of Lawrence and Broadway, home of the Green Mill Cocktail Lounge. From across the street, Rich saw Mr. Fox walk into the bar. Rich couldn't remember the last time he was in a bar, let alone the Green Mill. It had to have been years. From the outside, the bar looked exactly as he remembered it, glowing green marquee and all. He decided he might as well go in for a drink, or something else.

Rich found the bar unchanged on the inside. It had the same strange look and feel, like someplace that belonged more to the East Side than to the North. There was the same antique steel cash register, the same rickety stage, the same dim lighting. He thought he recognized the bartender as being the same man who'd once served him that disgusting double Manhattan years ago, when he'd sat at the bar with Francesca. Rich realized he was just as soaked from the rain now as he had been back then.

Mr. Fox was nowhere to be found, so Rich bellied up to the bar. The place was busy for so early in the night. From the stage, a trio played a jazz number. The bar clapped softly with the music, but the trio played for only a few minutes. After they'd finished, the stage was cleared of everything but a single stool and a microphone, which shone under a spotlight.

The bar quieted as a young girl stepped up to the stage. She looked ridiculous, wearing a fake white curly beard and a dingy old Cubs hat. After her eyes found Rich at the bar, she began.

I was a hero.

Name's Templeton Goodfellow, once the fine fellow, inventor of limoncello.

You'd think an old-as-Moses elf like me would have countless stories, but I don't. I have just one. We all have just one. It might be the story of a mother, father, queen, king, or hero (like me). It might be a sad story, or a happy one. The story might have happened in a night, a week, or a year. It might be a story no one cares to hear. But we all have the one story. There is only that one, despite all the stories you think you have.

My own story is one of those unbelievable stories you just have to believe.

It starts and ends with Maria de' Medici. I found the little princess by chance, in the middle of a strawberry field under a lemon tree, in the middle of the Middle Ages, when all there were were kingdoms, like this here city on the lake.

I prefer a kingdom. They're original, like her.

I was surprised to see Maria picking lemons, and not strawberries. I asked her why she picked such a sour fruit in the middle of a field with the sweetest. She said she made a special drink from the lemons. It was a drink that made you dizzy, she said. I told her I knew all about drinks that made you dizzy, so let me have a try. She gave me some of her lemon drink, and it tasted like water from the fountain of youth. We ended up drinking her drink and playing her childish games in the field all that day. I found she was not so different from me, only beautiful.

By sunset, I was so dizzy, I could hardly stand. She had to carry me home with her. She put me in a wicker basket of lemons and skipped the whole way back. It was bumpy, but I didn't mind. I could see her face from where she held me. It was a lovely view.

Maria lived as a princess in a fabulous castle, and I moved in with her there. I became her tutor, servant, jester, and playmate. I never played so much in my life. We played stick combat, barley break, and chess. The chess we played every night before bed. I slept in a candleholder on an old powder puff on her headboard. That powder puff was the most comfortable thing I ever slept on. I sang her a bedtime song from that puff. I sang a stout, a draught, a bout of gout. A dream is no dream without her about.

One Christmas, a great feast was held in the great hall. At the feast, we played king of the bean, a game where a small bean is baked inside a cake, and the one who finds it in their portion is crowned king of the holiday feast. Maria found the bean and was delighted, until her father, ever the cockshire, broke her golden heart. He told her a princess could not be king, but she could be married to one, and she WOULD be married to one. Right then and there, he announced to everyone that he had arranged for her to marry a king of a neighboring kingdom, some decades older than her and with balls no doubt grayer than the castle walls. But that sort of thing was customary back then. Still, Maria was sick with the thought of it. I was sicker than her. Christmas was ruined!

We tried to escape from the castle that night but were caught at the gates, betrayed by the white eyes of the moon. The poor girl was locked high in a prison keep with nothing to eat or drink, not until she agreed to the marriage. I knew she would never. I knew she would be skin and bones before agreeing to whore herself out.

I knew I must save her.

I was locked in a high prison keep myself, but escaped easily out the window, aboard the back of a crow friend of mine, who was nice enough to take a shit on the guards who had caught us, for good measure. As soon as I landed, I began in the design of a grand plan to rescue Maria. I had it in my head it would be one of those legendary princess rescues. There would be dash in the attack, a narrow escape, and, of course, a hero (me). That's how I had it in my head, at least. Things turned out differently.

As I was planning the rescue, I drank a glass of red wine. Then another. The planning was stressful business, so I had several more glasses after that. Before I knew it, I was three sheets to invincibility, hellfire in my eyes, crossbow in my hand, scaling the stairs to Maria's lockup. At her prison door, I shot the sleeping guard's eyeball out of his head with an arrow. He was lucky I missed. I'd been aiming for his jiggling-bone.[6]

I stole the guard's key, then a kiss from Maria. She suffocated my little head with more kisses as she carried me down the castle stairs and into the night. We would have been caught running out through the castle gates had the moon not been blinded by a heavy cloud. Rota Fortunae.

---

[6] *Dickie ding dong / groin snake / joystick / penis.*

My "plan" had fallen into place perfectly. I'd saved her.

Maria said it was a brilliant princess rescue. She said I was so brave. She said I was her knight in shining armor. She said I smelled like wine. She said I was a great shot with the crossbow.

She said I was her hero.

That night, sleeping in the woods, I had one of those strange midsummer night's dreams, no doubt brought on by the copious amount of wine. I dreamed I could fly, and I was flying Maria to somewhere young, somewhere dreams still come true, if they ever did come true. It was just me and Maria. We dropped trou, told the earth below and Thanatos behind to kiss our beautiful bare asses, and went flying through the ether. We drank a drink while we flew, a drink of lemons, like the drink she made. The drink was a spirit. And that made perfect sense, because spirits fly. We were flying together somewhere through heaven and felt the same as we'd been when we were six years old. Sweet lemony spirits for the flying six-year-old spirits.

When I woke, I didn't know it. I thought for a second maybe this was all the continuation of a dream, and maybe, just maybe, we were all still asleep. Dream or not, I knew I'd miss her when I was gone, and we were, whatever we were …

I think it was a flight of spirits.

The bartender poured flight glasses of spirits for the few people seated around the bar, including Rich. Rich stared into the bottom of his glass, then drained it silently to the health of Templeton, who he knew from the story must have passed away, or maybe flown away.

A gust of wind snuck through a crack in the bar's front window. It was the last breath of the storm. Color faded from the sky outside, but the city shined on. A new band prepared on the stage, and the seats started to fill. The night was just beginning. Rich wondered what it had in store for him. He set the empty glass down and looked up at himself in the mirror behind the bar. He thought he looked younger in the dark light. He thought he looked not so different from the boy he had been the last time he'd looked in that mirror, which gave him the strange sensation of time's passing backward. There was something of a twinkle in his eye, and as he wondered at the twinkling, he saw Francesca Finnegan approaching from the other end of the bar, near the stage. She looked as she always had, not a day older than when he'd last seen her. She pulled up a barstool next to him and smiled. He smiled back. She asked him a simple question, her favorite question, a question Rich hadn't been asked since he was a boy.

"What's your favorite color?"

Acknowledgements

Thanks to Chris Cihon, the brilliant artist responsible for all of the illustrations in this book. Chris completed this story, in pictures.

The writing in this book was beautifully improved and edited by Jen McDonald. Thank you Jen for taking on such a strange project. You can learn more about Jen at jenbmcdonald.com.

Thanks mom, for everything. Thanks dad, for *The Sad Chapter*.

Trevor McCormack. You, sir, would have to be the Lavender Line conductor.

Last but not least, Kellan, Francesca, and Jenny. This is our story.

Works Cited

Allingham, William. "The Fairies." In *Irish Songs and Poems*. London: Longmans, Green and Company, 1901.

Corgan, Billy. *Tonight, Tonight*. On *Mellon Collie and the Infinite Sadness*. Smashing Pumpkins. © 1995 by Virgin.

Gurnon, Emily. "Ice from Michigan Ave. Building Falls, Kills Man." *Chicago Tribune*, March 1, 1994. http://articles.chicagotribune.com/1994-03-01/news/9403010211_1_four-story-building-neiman-marcus-john-hancock-center.

Joyce, James. *Finnegans Wake*. London: Faber and Faber, 1939.

Ocasek, Ric. *Magic*. On *Heartbeat City*. The Cars. © 1984 by Elektra.

Schneider, Ben. *The Birds are Singing at Night*. On *A Walk in the Woods*. Lord Huron. © 2015 by Varese Sarabande.

William Shakespeare, *A Midsummer Night's Dream*, in *A Midsummer Night's Dream and Other Comedies*, Ann Arbor, Michigan, Borders Classics, 2007.

Steve Wiley, Author

Steve is a father, husband, uncle, brother, friend, and purveyor of fairy stories. He grew up in and around Chicagoland, where he still lives with his wife and two kids. He has been published in an array of strange and serious places,  from the U.S. Chamber of Commerce in Washington, D.C., to *Crannóg* magazine in Galway, Ireland. This is his first book. He has an undergraduate degree in something he has forgotten from Illinois State University and a graduate degree in something equally forgotten from DePaul University. You can email Steve at Lavenderlinepress@gmail.com, or visit *thewileymancan* on Instagram.

Chris Cihon, Illustrator

Chris is an artist who studied at Columbia College Chicago. He is a Chicago native and has lived here all his life. Chris's paintings have been showcased in many local galleries and beyond. When he feels like it, he travels elsewhere to find inspiration.

You can reach him at Chris.cihon@gmail.com, or visit _ccihon_ on Instagram.

CPSIA information can be obtained
at www.ICGtesting.com
Printed in the USA
LVOW13*1418040417
529576LV00011B/208/P